Rory zeroed in
and the ball in

"Oh, wow! Are these
and his freckles standing out against his pale face.

"They are. And it's still light enough for us to try them out," Seth said, glancing at Lila, who moved at a much slower pace toward the steps.

She shifted her purse to the other shoulder and seemed to take in everything before stepping up. "Oh...oh...that rosebush is beautiful. Where did it come from?" She brushed past her son, who turned to spot what she was exclaiming over.

"I passed a nursery after I left the sporting-goods store. The rose called to me," Seth said, deliberately making light of the agony he went through to choose it.

"It's perfect there," she said, her eyes shiny with tears. "I don't know why I never thought to buy something to decorate the porch. It's the very touch needed to greet guests. I've no idea what it cost, Seth, but you must let me reimburse you."

"The rose is a gift."

Dear Reader,

I've been to Montana and have set books there before, so my fictional town of Snowy Owl Crossing has characteristics of other ranching towns I've traveled through. As in all small communities, it's the people who live and work there that make it a place you'd want to visit and maybe even settle down. It's the same in *A Maverick's Heart*.

Seth Maxwell came for his brother's wedding, liked the area and was drawn to Lila Jenkins, owner of the B and B where he rents a room. Seth has never set down roots, instead traveling to exotic places finding and selling precious and semiprecious gems.

Lila, a widow with a nine-year-old son, has deep roots in Snowy Owl Crossing. She struggles to hang on to the Owl's Nest, which she bought before her husband died in a mine collapse. A mine where Seth has heard previous gem hunters found sapphires.

Ah, can you see rocks, not gems, along the road to Seth and Lila falling in love? I hope you enjoy their story. As in *His Ranch or Hers*, my depiction of the snowy owls is tied to the group of friends who wants to ensure a habitat for the birds that long ago arrived and originally took up residence in abandoned eagles' nests, some returning year after year.

As always I love hearing from readers via mail at 7739 E. Broadway Blvd #101, Tucson, AZ 85710-3941, or email at rdfox@cox.net.

Sincerely,

Roz Denny Fox

A MAVERICK'S HEART

ROZ DENNY FOX

HARLEQUIN® WESTERN ROMANCE®

ISBN-13: 978-0-373-75627-8

A Maverick's Heart

This edition published by arrangement with Harlequin Books S.A.

For questions and comments about the quality of this book, please contact us at CustomerService@Harlequin.com.

Printed in U.S.A.

Roz Denny Fox's first book was published by Harlequin in 1990. She writes for several Harlequin lines and her books are published worldwide in a number of languages. Roz's warm home-and-family-focused love stories have been nominated for various industry awards, including the Romance Writers of America's RITA® Award, the Holt Medallion, the Golden Quill and others. Roz has been a member of the Romance Writers of America since 1987 and is currently a member of Tucson's Saguaro Romance Writers, where she has received the Barbara Award for outstanding chapter service. In 2013 Roz received her fifty-book pin from Harlequin. Readers can email her through Facebook or at rdfox@cox.net, or visit her website at korynna.com/rozfox.

Books by Roz Denny Fox

Harlequin American Romance

The Maverick Returns
Duke: Deputy Cowboy
Texas Dad
Texas Mom
His Ranch or Hers

Harlequin Heartwarming

Annie's Neighborhood
An Unlikely Rancher
Molly's Garden

Visit the Author Profile page
at Harlequin.com for more titles.

I'd like to dedicate this story to the wonderful gem people who put on the Tucson Gem and Mineral Show every year. The more years I attend, the more I love seeing gems and minerals from all over the world.

Chapter One

Lila Jenkins bustled around the Snowy Owl Café, straightening up after her women's group, the Artsy Ladies, ended their meeting. "Rory," she called to her nine-year-old son. He was in the kitchen with his grandmother. "Collect your homework and bring your backpack. It's almost time to go home."

The lanky kid dragged his pack into the café. "Mom, tomorrow can I go to ball practice? Coach told Kemper if I watch, I'll learn what Little Leaguers do."

She paused. "It's supposed to rain. If so, won't the coach cancel practice again?"

Three of the women who'd been at the meeting said goodbye. Tawana Whitefeather still stood at the kitchen pass-through chatting with Lila's mother.

Waving to those leaving, Lila still saw her son's pout that ran his many cheek freckles together. "I'm never gonna get to play ball on Kemper's team, am I?"

"Well, I asked Kemper's dad about costs. We're earning some extra money what with Zeke Maxwell's brother and his other friends staying at our B and B for Zeke's wedding. I may be able to swing the fees."

He perked right up. "Yippee!"

Lila chewed her bottom lip. "It's not yippee-time yet, Rory. You need new equipment. And with games being in Wolf Point, there's a matter of transportation."

"I can ride my bike," he said brightly.

"No way. You're only to ride your bike from the school to Memaw's café. Don't even think about riding farther. I'll pay gas for someone to drive you. But, honey, cash is still tight, so for now it's only a maybe."

Rory's shoulders slumped. "I wish my daddy hadn't died," he mumbled. "He'd buy baseball stuff for me and teach me to bat and catch and throw like Kemper and his daddy."

"Oh, sweetie, I'm sorry, too. I'll do my best to work something out." Crossing to him, Lila tried to kiss his thick auburn waves, but he ducked. With a light brush of his cowlick, she finished wiping the last table then joined Tawana.

"Lila, what time is Zeke's brother taking the other groomsmen to the airport?"

"All I know is they're checking out after breakfast."

"Did Hunter ask about booking a room? He's planning to come back after he gets his permanent prosthetic leg."

Glancing at her friend, Lila reeled a bit, but hoped she hid her envy. First, Myra had found someone to love. Now, Tawana may have met someone special.

The pretty Native American feigned innocence. “Didn’t I mention he and I plan to keep in touch? We hope to meet in DC if Jewell gets us an appointment to see the Natural Resource Committee about our snowy owl preserve. Hunter’s VA is near there. Well, it’s late. I’d better run. Thanks for providing a meeting place, Doreen,” she called through the opening.

“I love having you all while I wait for my dough to rise. I have four pans of cinnamon rolls ready for the morning rush. Now I can lock up and go up to bed.”

“It’s raining again,” Rory announced. He had his face pressed to the glass of the front door.

“Drive carefully, you two,” Doreen said. “Rain makes roads slick.” She came out of the kitchen.

Lila skirted Tawana to hug her mother. “Don’t worry, Mom. You know all the ranchers in the area are asleep by now. We’ll be the only ones on the highway.”

Tawana picked up the sweatshirt she’d worn into the diner. “Yuk. Still wet.”

“You have the farthest to drive,” Doreen said. “I’ll run upstairs and get you a loaner. You can return it next time you’re in town.”

“I’ll go, Mom.” So saying, Lila dashed off.

Doreen went to the door. Reaching over her grandson, she slid open the dead bolt.

“Auntie Tawana, are you going home with Mama and me?” Rory gazed expectantly at one of his faux aunts.

She laughed. “No, slugger. I have my pickup.” She

accepted the fresh sweatshirt from Lila, who had reappeared.

"Mama, she called me 'slugger.'" Rory beamed. "Did you tell everybody how much I want to play baseball?"

"Honey bunny, like you didn't tell everyone within earshot at Auntie Myra's wedding reception."

"Oh, yeah." His grin widened, but he looked a bit sheepish. "Some of the men there asked why Kemper and me want to play ball instead of ride in the kids' rodeo. Why do they think rodeo is funner?"

"More fun, not funner, Rory. And it's Kemper and I, not me," Lila corrected as they readied to follow Tawana outside.

"Well, we have more pro rodeo riders than baseball players in these parts," Doreen said. "It's something to consider."

Rory's face fell again.

Seeing his crestfallen expression, Lila rose to his defense. "Mama, I'm all for him choosing what he wants to do. Most schools have ball teams. Anyway, by the time he's grown, who knows what he'll want to do."

"True." Doreen nodded. "I want Rory to be happy, but I especially want him to stay out of the mines."

"Lord, yes." Lila didn't need the subtle reminder that her dad and her husband had both died in mine accidents. "G'night. Wait, Ma…do you need me to work the breakfast shift? I could use the time to wash linens and tidy the rooms. Three of the guys are checking out of the Owl's Nest tomorrow and

I've got two couples who stayed with me last year booked for trout fishing this weekend. I need to turn the rooms around fast."

"Take the morning off. Tell the fishermen if they catch any, I'll buy them to serve as a weekend dinner special."

Lila flipped up her hood. "Okay, but they may be catch-and-release fishermen."

"If not, my offer's on the table."

Doreen closed up as Lila skipped over a deep puddle to unlock her old Jeep Cherokee, making sure Tawana's pickup had started before she climbed in.

"What's 'catch and release'?" Rory asked once he settled into the backseat on the passenger side. It was always his chosen spot.

She checked to see he'd buckled in before firing the engine. "There are people who love to fish, but either don't want to see fish die or they have no means of keeping them fresh to cook. So they turn them back into the lake or river."

"Um, I guess that's good. But it seems silly."

Lila smiled as she left the town behind. "Fly-fishing takes skill. And let's not say anything negative, since fishermen rent our rooms and that pays our bills."

"Okay. I'm tired. How long before we get home?"

Lila heard his yawn. "Ten or fifteen minutes."

Rory fell silent and Lila thought he had gone to sleep—which left her free to worry about whether she was a bad mother for making him stay with her at work. Since kindergarten, Kemper Barnes had been Rory's best friend. Rory used to go home with him to play or to study until the café closed and Lila could pick him up. Now that Kemper was in Little League, Rory had to come to the café. And on nights she met with the Artsy Ladies, he was stuck there late.

As she'd told her mom, the highway was empty tonight. It wasn't long before she turned onto the paved lane that led to their ranch.

Suddenly Rory shouted, "Mom, stop! You're going to hit Ghost and…and a man!"

Her nerves jangled—she'd thought Rory was asleep. His shout had her stomping hard on the brake pedal as she glimpsed a flash of white off to her right. The Cherokee hit a puddle of standing water, and although she'd slowed for the turn, she felt the front end kite. Her back wheels spun like racing slicks seconds before the brakes grabbed. It all happened so fast and jerkily, her head smacked the left-side window hard. Briefly all went dim and she heard birds tweeting and bees buzzing.

Lila wanted to clutch her head. Instead she gripped the wheel tighter. Only vaguely did she remain aware that the back end of her SUV had landed in a deep culvert.

Flinching, Lila wondered why her lights cast pretty halos in the branches of a nearby tree instead of illuminating the lane ahead of her. She tried to check on Rory, but a sharp pain in her head rendered her voiceless.

All at once her door was yanked open. The dome light illuminated the SUV's interior, blinding Lila. Ghost, the almost-white yellow Lab that Jewell Hyatt had given Rory after his dad died, scrambled across her tense body and over into the backseat.

"Are you okay?" inquired a deep male voice.

Somewhere behind her Lila heard her son ordering his dog to stop licking him. A tiny bit of her relaxed. However, she honestly didn't know whether she should tell the man yes, she was okay, or no, she might be dead and floating above everything amid those sparkly lights.

But she wasn't dead. She felt the man's arm slide across her, saw him put the Jeep in Park and turn the key to shut off the engine. Then his head appeared directly in front of her still-unfocused eyes. Blond hair, askew. Darker in spots from the rain. Gorgeous yet concerned green eyes in a chiseled, sun-bronzed face stared at her. Well-shaped lips set in a straight line above an appealing cleft in his manly chin.

It took Lila several rocketing heartbeats, but she finally managed to assemble all the attractive parts from those strong shoulders upward. The parts belonged to Seth Maxwell, Myra's husband's twin, who was staying on after his brother's wedding. He'd been the groomsman who'd escorted Lila down the aisle.

He shone a small, bright light in her eyes, causing her to wince and blink, and she lost his handsomeness into blackness shot with pinpoints of pain.

Rory's anxious voice yelling, "Mom… Mom!" right near her ear shook Lila from her stupor as nothing else had.

She tried once more to speak, but her mouth felt as if she'd swallowed cotton.

"Is my mom all right?" she heard Rory demand.

SETH MAXWELL FROWNED. "I don't know, kid. For sure she's dazed. I need to get her to the house so we can see. I'll carry her if you can manage the dog—the rascal. I took him out for a run. When he spotted your car, he yanked the leash right out of my hand. I was scared witless that your car would hit him."

"Me, too," Rory said. "I don't think Mom saw him or you. I yelled at her to stop. I probably made us land in the ditch."

"If anyone's to blame, it's me. I took your dog out in questionable weather," Seth assured the boy as he shifted the flashlight to his left hand and with his right slowly released Lila's seat belt. "I'm going to get your mom. We'll take it slow back to the house, okay?"

"The lane goes straight there," Rory said. "What were you doing with Ghost anyway?"

"Ghost?" Seth, confused, paused in lifting Lila into his arms.

"My dog. He stays in our part of the house when we're gone."

"Well, tonight he was in the foyer. I wanted to go for a run and your dog brought me his leash."

Rory tightened his grip on that leash. "Oh, you're one of the guys renting from us, huh?"

"Yes. Remember, we met at my brother's wedding? Most of the guys in the wedding party are staying here until tomorrow. Tonight we all went to Zeke's place for supper. He and his wife fed us so well, when I got home and realized the rain had slackened, I decided to go out for exercise." Seth spoke calmly to the boy as he trudged toward the house with his burden. "In the middle of our run it started to drizzle, so I turned back."

Lila spoke for the first time, a guttural sound somewhere below Seth's chin. "I, uh, think I can walk." She gingerly touched her left temple. "I hit my head on something. Maybe the window. Did I crack it?"

"Your head?" Seth asked, a smile in his voice.

Lila shoved at his solid shoulder. "The window, you goose. Did I break the window?"

"No, but you did a number on your vehicle. It's stuck. We need daylight to see if you did any damage to its underpinnings. I don't think you broke an axle," he said, supporting her back with his hand.

"My head hurts, but stuff is starting to make sense. Rory, we carry a big flashlight in the glove box. Run back and get it for Mr. Maxwell."

"It's Seth, okay?" They'd all stopped in the lane, and Rory and Ghost ran back to the Cherokee, leaving Seth and Lila in the dark.

"Since I'm hanging around at your B and B a month or so to help Zeke roof his barn," Seth said, "can't we use first names?"

He let go of Lila to take the flashlight the boy had slogged back with. She buckled and Seth snatched her up before she fell to her knees.

"Sorry," she murmured. "My legs don't seem to want to hold me."

"Probably nerves," Seth said matter-of-factly, scooping her up. "Rory, you take the bigger light. It's enough. Let's go. I'll be right behind you, carrying your mom."

"Why can't she walk? Does she need a doctor? Mom, you're not gonna die, are you?" The kid froze and Seth almost bowled him over.

She gripped the front of Seth's jacket. "I need to walk on my own," she insisted. "This is ridiculous. I wasn't going very fast when I made the turn. How could sliding into the ditch muddle my brain?"

"Even minor accidents can throw a person off-kilter. We're almost at the house. Rory, walk on with the light. Once we get inside we'll make sure your mom's all right."

The boy did as directed, letting Ghost bound up to the front door and shake off his wet coat. The others followed in rapid succession.

Once inside Seth headed for the dining room, where he'd spent the most time besides his rented bedroom in the big old farmhouse. For having been here almost a week since his twin's wedding, he'd seen remarkably little of Lila Jenkins. They'd been paired up in the wedding party. His initial impression had been of an attractive, petite woman who looked exceptionally good in an old-fashioned wine-red dress. She'd hurried away right after the ceremony to appear again in a black skirt, white blouse and white apron at the reception, where she and an older woman served the meal and helped hand out cake and punch. No matter which outfit Lila'd had on, she'd gained his interest.

He'd danced with several of his new sister-in-law's friends, but he'd only caught glimpses of Lila, who by then seemed to be part of a two-woman cleanup crew.

Even at her bed-and-breakfast, she remained elusive. Breakfast was the only meal included in the rental fee, and they always found it hot and inviting, served in covered silver dishes on a sideboard.

Zeke's wife, Myra, had told him Lila had a son and a dog, as well as horses that were available to rent. But because Hunter Wright, another of Zeke's army buddies, had a temporary prosthesis, they'd elected to drive around to see as much of Montana and its fishing holes as they could cram into the short time the three guys had to visit.

Seth's pal Gavin had joked that they must be renting from elves who supplied a scrumptious breakfast, made beds and replaced used towels while the guests were out. Ben Archer, who Zeke called Sarge, said maybe the old house came with ghosts he occasionally heard padding around the lower floors. At the time none of them had known the dog's name was Ghost. Seth couldn't wait to tell them what they might learn if they didn't retire so early.

With his foot he dragged out one of the padded dining chairs and started to set Lila down.

"Why are you bringing me in here?" she asked. "Never mind. I can walk into the kitchen on my own." She levered herself up with one hand on the table and the other on Seth's arm.

Rory had unclipped Ghost's leash and Seth could hear the dog lapping water in the next room.

"Where's the kitchen light switch?" Seth asked, steadying Lila as she moved toward the dark doorway.

"I'll get it," Rory called, dashing ahead. "Mom, are you feeling better? Is your head cracked open?" Flipping on the light, he shrugged out of a backpack Seth hadn't noticed before.

"I'm fine, son." Lila reached for a teakettle sitting atop an old stove. "I'll fix some tea. Uh, thanks, Mr—uh, Seth. It's more I feel like an idiot for landing in a ditch. I know every turn in that road. I've never done anything like that before." She filled the kettle, set it on a burner and turned it on. Her movements were jerky, even as she nervously raked a hand through her short dark hair.

Seth saw her wince and he frowned. "Here, let me take a look at your head. Maybe I should run you to the emergency room."

"Good heavens, no." Lila braced her hands on the counter, but tipped her head forward so Seth could get a clear look.

"No blood. That's good," he said.

"Ouch." Lila pushed away Seth's exploring fingers.

"You have some swelling a couple of inches above your left ear." Seth gently separated strands of her hair. And since he was so much taller he was able to get a good look without hurting her again. "Do you have any ice?"

"I'll get it, okay, Mom? Will that make your head

well?" Rory asked, darting across the room to a big refrigerator.

"Ice will be good." Lila sat in a kitchen chair and actually smiled at Seth. "Ice will be very good if it'll make you guys stop acting like I'm knocking on death's door. Rory, you need to go to bed. Tomorrow's a school day. And, Seth, probably you, too, since you're driving your friends to the airport in the morning. Before it gets much later, I should phone one of my neighbors with a tractor to see if someone can run over here early and pull the Cherokee out of the ditch. Preferably a neighbor who won't blab all over town and worry my mother," she said more to herself than to the others.

Rory brought her a plastic bag filled with ice, and the dog trotted beside him. "Memaw said she likes that everybody comes into the café to gossip. She finds out all the good stuff that way."

Chuckling, Seth took the ice bag before the kid plopped it too hard against his mother's head. He picked up a dish towel and wrapped the bag, telling the boy, "This towel will cushion your mom's head against freezing and sharp ice cube edges."

"Gosh, you know a lot about doctoring bumps." Rory ran his fingers through the dog's fur and gazed at the man in awe.

"I hunt gemstones in a lot of remote spots where I can get scratches or bumps and bruises. Often it's only me to take care of myself."

The kettle whistled and Lila started to get up, but he placed a hand on her shoulder. "Don't get up. I'll fix your tea." He moved the kettle and shut off the burner.

"You don't have to do that. I should be asking if you want coffee or anything since that's what you pay me for."

"I pay you for a room, with breakfast thrown in." He opened a cupboard and luck was with him. Cups were stacked in neat rows. He took one down and spotted a line of canisters. One read Tea. Pulling out a bag, he set it in the cup and poured the water.

"Rory, to bed," Lila said. "I'm feeling much improved. Once I drink a cup of tea, I'll be right as rain."

"You and Memaw always say that. How right is rain if it made our car go in a ditch?"

"It's an expression," Lila told him. "I don't know where it comes from. Ghost can sleep in your room tonight. Brush your teeth and crawl into bed. I'll pop by and turn out your light shortly, honey."

"Okay. Mr. Seth, will you stay and make sure she's okay? She cut her hand on the meat slicer at the café and wouldn't see a doctor. She got poisoned blood and Memaw yelled at her."

"Blood poisoning," Lila corrected, indicating a spot on the table where Seth could set her steaming cup. "It was during rodeo week. We were swamped at the café. I didn't see the red streaks up my arm at first. But I healed, Rory."

"Yeah. Okay. Come on, Ghost."

Lila beckoned him with her free arm and although he cast an uncomfortable glance at Seth, the boy stepped into his mom's arm for a hug. "G'nite." He grabbed the dog's collar, aimed a wave at Seth and the two loped out of the kitchen.

"You really don't need to babysit me," Lila told Seth, holding the ice bag to her head with one hand. With her free hand she removed a cell phone from the small purse still draped across her body.

"Let me call Zeke for you," Seth said. "He has a winch on the front of his pickup. I'm sure he'll be discreet." He dug out his phone.

"Zeke's on his honeymoon," Lila reminded him. "Sort of..." she added as she took a sip of tea.

Grinning, Seth hit a speed-dial number and put the phone on speaker. "Hey, bro... Lila put her Jeep in the ditch right as you turn into her place."

"Is she okay?"

"I think so. I said you'd bring your truck over bright and early tomorrow morning. The guys and I can help you winch it out before we head to the airport. She didn't want me to ask you since you're supposed to be on your honeymoon."

The man at the other end of the call snorted. "If you come over and learn ranching, dude, we'd leave you in charge so Myra and I could get away for a week."

"I'd need a crash course in cows, buddy. Hey, what's Myra saying? I hear her talking in the background."

"She wants to know if Lila or Rory got hurt."

"Rory's fine. Lila—" Seth started to mention her lump, but she grabbed his arm and shook her head. "I, uh, went running with their dog," Seth said instead. "He got away from me. Lila had to brake hard to keep from colliding with us and her car slid into the ditch. That's all."

Lila juggled the melting ice bag and took another drink of tea.

Seth finished making arrangements with his twin then clicked off. "You heard? Zeke said he'll pop by at first light, before morning chores."

"Thanks. I appreciate you handling that for me."

"It's nothing."

"It's something to me. I've been the one to deal with everything…well, it'll soon be five years."

Seth waited for her to elaborate. He knew that she ran this place alone, but he hadn't heard why. He assumed she was divorced, but the moment passed before he could ask.

"Like I told Rory, I'm okay. You can go on to bed. I'll finish my tea then check on him and call it a night, too. Tomorrow's breakfast is my mom's special coffee cake, plus scrambled eggs with crumbled bacon. It'll be ready by seven."

Taking the hint that she wanted him to get lost, Seth moved the ice bag first to check her head one more time. The swelling had receded. "Yep, you're almost back to normal." He feathered his fingers through her hair and let them trail down her cheek.

Pulling back warily, she exclaimed, "I told you so!"

He watched her sitting there stoically a moment longer and was intrigued enough to want to learn more about his lovely landlady. By staying on, he'd have time to dig a little deeper. Since college he'd never stuck in one place for long. Much about this small Montana town left him longing to sink roots.

Stepping back, Seth offered a last smile then headed for the door. He called over his shoulder, "I'll set my alarm and roust Ben and Gavin to go along to help Zeke. You set up one of your great breakfasts and leave rescuing the Cherokee to us."

She started to object and he retreated fast.

But maybe it was time she had someone around to give her a hand. Maybe he'd be that someone.

From the first time his twin had called to tell him about the ranch he'd been given by the folks of a kid he'd saved in Afghanistan, Seth envied his brother the joy he'd found here in Snowy Owl Crossing. Maybe it was time he cut back on his footloose lifestyle.

Chapter Two

Early the next morning Seth hustled his new friends up and out of the B and B before breakfast, explaining that they were going to rescue their landlady's vehicle from a ditch.

"Did I miss how it is you know about Miz Lila's car?" Gavin Denton asked around a wide yawn as they set off down the lane.

"I didn't say. Guilt, probably, because I'm more or less to blame."

"So that explains why you're all fired up on us helping at the crack of dawn," Ben Archer remarked, dropping back to walk with Hunter Wright, the third man in their party. They'd all served as Zeke Maxwell's groomsmen. Seth had expressly told Hunter he didn't need to come along this morning, since he hadn't fully mastered walking well on his temporary prosthetic leg. But as with everything else they'd done throughout the week, Hunter adamantly refused special treatment.

"Okay, give us the real story." Gavin prodded Seth. "Now I'm curious."

"I told you I was going for a run after dinner." Seth relayed how he'd taken the Jenkinses' family dog along. "We were returning home when the dog saw their car. He tore loose from me. Lila or her son must have seen him. She swerved and that sent her into the ditch."

"I guess she wasn't hurt," Ben ventured. "At least as we trouped downstairs I smelled something good cooking. Hey…what about her kid?"

"He's fine. She smacked her head on the driver's side window and suffered a fair-size goose egg. Stubborn lady agreed to an ice pack, but wouldn't let me take her to the emergency room." Seth scowled as he admitted that last bit.

"Why didn't you wake us? Maybe collectively we could've convinced her to see a doc. It sounds as if you think she should have," Gavin said.

Ben laughed. "Gav, how many women do you know who can be moved once their mind is made up?"

Gavin shrugged. "I can't recall ever trying to move one."

Their party reached the vehicle, ending the discussion of women.

"Hot damn, she's stuck, all right," Ben announced then issued a whistle as he walked to the back of the mired Cherokee.

"It actually looks worse this morning." Seth crouched to inspect the SUV's cantilevered rear. "Last night I figured only the back left tire went into the culvert, but now I see both did."

Hunter Wright paced over and leaned heavily on his cane. "You can see skid marks where she probably braked hard after entering this low spot where there's still standing water. The fact both tires went into the muck will make extracting it with your brother's winch easier."

"You think so?" Seth rose to stand beside Hunter.

"I'd trust Hunt's opinion," Ben said. "But maybe nobody told you he's an engineer."

"Was," Hunter stressed. "Before I went into the military."

Seth took another look at the injured man. "Zeke only said you were all in the same unit in Iraq then got split up but kept in contact. I'd think engineering would be a field you could return to now that you've left the service."

The man leaning on the cane gazed into the distance. "My dad and brother own a firm in New Jersey. I'm not sure I could fit back in. I only worked there a year before opting out to join the military. And my orthopedic surgeon at Walter Reed says I need at least one, maybe two, more surgeries on the leg." He tapped his hip above the missing limb. "I envy you getting to stay here longer, Seth. It's pretty much God's country. Do you think you'll do like Zeke and settle down here?"

Surprised by the question, Seth shrugged. "Part of me hankers to stay put. But I've got to travel the globe for work. It's all I've ever done since leaving college. I don't know how I'd support myself if I wasn't searching for gems."

Gavin, who'd circled the whole vehicle, arrived back at the group in the middle of Seth's lament. "What about going after sapphires in some of Montana's abandoned mines? Sapphires are pricey gems, right?"

Seth gaped at him. "Real sapphires?"

"I assume so," Gavin said. "When Zeke phoned to ask if I could get leave to be in his wedding, I didn't know a blessed thing about Montana. So I did some internet research. Sounds like there's sapphires as well as gold and copper mines. Some of them are near here, but I don't know if they're operating. If Zeke can't tell you, you could ask some of the old-timers we met at his wedding reception."

"Speaking of the newlywed," Ben interrupted, "here he comes. Let's rib him about not wanting to leave his bed—so he makes us stand around waiting for him to show up."

"Skip the teasing," Hunter warned. "His wife is with him."

Indeed, Myra jumped out of the pickup as soon as Zeke stopped. "Where's Lila?" she asked, glancing around. "This looks bad. Was she hurt? I thought you told Zeke she was okay," she challenged Seth. "It's not like her to not be out here supervising."

"There's no need for her to come out," Seth shot back. "I told her the guys and I would help Zeke rescue her vehicle."

"Zeke," she called, "I'm going to run up to the house to check on Lila. She sometimes tends to be too stoic for her own good."

Her husband nodded. "This shouldn't take long. Don't get too wrapped up talking to Lila about what all you missed at last night's Artsy Ladies meeting." Grinning, Zeke winked at Myra even as he unhooked the cable on the winch.

"I'll be quick," she promised and jogged off.

"She had to miss a meeting to feed all of us last night?" Seth asked his brother.

"She didn't have to. She wanted to see you all again and thank you guys for showing up on such short notice to be in our wedding. Well, not you, Seth. You already had tickets to visit. But the others." He handed Seth the hook on the end of the cable and smiled at his groomsmen. "Damn, but I'm going to miss you guys all over again. Remember, any time you can take leave, ours is a revolving door. You, too, Hunter, once the docs get you squared away."

Gavin let out a big guffaw. "Don't you mean the door here at the Owl's Nest revolves? It was clever how you prebooked us here."

Zeke didn't bother to look sheepish. "Hey, buddy," he said instead, "wait until you get married and see how many big dudes you want snoring all night on the other side of your bedroom wall."

"I was kidding." Gavin gave Zeke a friendly fist bump. "Shall we quit jawing and get this SUV unstuck? Or am I the only one tempted by the cinnamon smell of whatever goodies Miz Lila fixed today?" He sniffed the air. "My mouth's watering from here."

The others agreed and, outside of Hunter Wright, who moved out of the way but still offered insight on the best way to hook the cable to the mired auto's front axle, their teamwork made the retrieval short and easy.

Seth helped Zeke rewind the cable onto the winch then scanned the others. "I'm going to drive the Jeep to the house. Who wants a ride?"

"Do you have the key?" Ben asked.

"It's still in the ignition."

Zeke, who'd been about to climb into his pickup, stopped. "You left it in the ignition all night?"

Seth frowned. "It wasn't like anyone could climb in and drive it away. Don't forget it was rainy and dark, and I had a boy and dog to shepherd as well as carrying Lila, who was woozy after banging her head on the side window."

"What? She hit her head?" Zeke exclaimed. "Myra is gonna be pissed at you. You led us to believe she was A-OK."

"Yeah, well she let me know that wasn't something she wanted to get around and worry her mother. She had a small knot, but the skin wasn't broken."

"Boy, Myra's probably going to say it could've been a concussion."

Seth shrugged. All at once Ben and Gavin, standing near the front of the Cherokee, ducked and flung their arms over their heads. One of them shouted, "Hey, cripes! Incoming! What the hell is that?"

The air stirred as a large bird dived talons first into the culvert and rose again with a screeching rodent. A second, slightly smaller, all-white bird circled above the dumbstruck quintet of men, crying, *pyee-pyee, pyee-pyee* right before the pair flew off.

"Wow." Zeke was first to break the silence. "Those were snowy owls, guys. The male made off with a good-size rat."

By then the others had sufficiently recovered from their initial shock to squint and follow the birds' flight.

Hunter shifted his stance. "What a sight. I'm glad we had this experience. From the way Myra's friend Tawana talked about how the owls return here every year to nest… I figured they'd already all gone north."

"Are they dangerous?" Gavin asked. "I think that second one grazed my head."

Zeke watched Gavin scrub a hand through his crew cut. "They don't attack humans, dude. They do rid our ranchlands of pests like mice, rats and voles. Myra and I had a tug-of-war with a huge male once who tried to make off with her minipig, Orion."

Ben muffled an expletive. "Not in your kitchen, right? Then again, who keeps a pig in their kitchen?"

Zeke socked his pal's arm. "Hey, a pet is a pet is a pet. And the day it happened, we had Orion in a pen outside near where we were cutting alfalfa. I told you last night…the little guy grows on you."

Wisely his friends held their tongues, although not all schooled their doubtful expressions.

"Orion is cute," Seth said, opening the Cherokee's door. "Hey, if we want any of that great-smelling breakfast before we leave for the airport, we'd better hop to it."

Ben and Gavin climbed into the backseat, leaving the front passenger seat for Hunter.

"I'm positive keeping a pig in any part of the house, especially the kitchen, wouldn't grow on me," Gavin asserted once they were inside the SUV and out of Zeke's hearing.

After starting the engine, Seth glanced behind him. "Is a pig any worse than goldfish or parrots or snakes?"

"Okay, I see your point. To each his own," Gavin muttered.

Hunter turned to address his one-time regiment buddies. "If any of us fell in love with a pig owner like Zeke did, we'd change our minds. Love short-circuits brain cells."

They all laughed as Seth parked near the entrance to the B and B.

The others piled out of the Cherokee. Without waiting for Zeke, all but Seth climbed the steps and went inside. He noticed Lila's son at the side of the building, tossing a baseball in the air. Even though the boy wore an old mitt on his left hand, he missed catching three times out of three. Ghost chased after the dropped ball and carried it back to the kid.

"Hiya, Rory," Seth called, pausing to lean on the handrail. "You need to teach Ghost to throw the ball back to you." He grinned. "Are you on a team or just goofing around?"

Rory took the ball from Ghost and wiped dog slobber on his pants, his shoulders sagging as he squinted at Seth. "I wanna join the team my best friend is on.

Mom first said it was too 'spensive. But last night she said she'll try to figure out how I can play. Were you in Little League when you were my age?"

"What's your age? Eight?"

"I'm nine," Rory said, puffing up his chest. "Since last month."

"Hmm. At nine I played on a junior boy's city league. In junior high, high school and college my brother and I were on school teams. Do you watch the pros? We grew up going to see the Boston Red Sox."

"That'd be cool. I like to watch games."

Zeke drove up, parked beside Lila's Cherokee and vaulted from his pickup. "Hi, Rory," he hollered. "Hey, did your mom finally sign you up for Little League?" he asked, bounding over to stand beside his twin.

"Not yet. And I'm not very good. Even if Mom finds money so I can join Kemper's team, I probably won't get to play in a real game."

Zeke clapped Seth on the back. "You should get this guy to give you tips while he's staying here. He racked up awards and trophies playing baseball. In college he had scouts after him. We all thought he'd end up in the majors. He was definitely good enough."

Before his brother or Rory could comment, the front door opened and Myra stepped out onto the porch. "There you guys are. Zeke, Lila invited us to join the men for breakfast here. It'll save us driving into town to the café and give you a last few minutes with your friends."

"That'd be great if it's no trouble for Lila." Zeke

hurried up the steps. He kissed Myra soundly even as she leaned over the porch rail to address Rory.

"Your mom says to bring Ghost and come get ready for school. It's supposed to be sunny, so she'll load your bike and you can ride to the café after school."

"Isn't there a cattlemen's meeting at the café today?" Zeke asked. "Is it lunch or supper?"

"The meeting starts at three. Probably more like supper by the time everyone orders and eats. Why?"

"I thought if it was a late lunch I'd eat more breakfast," Zeke said.

His brother swept by him and Myra. "You'd better get inside fast, dude. If your buds get a jump on us there'll only be crumbs left. Those three eat like there's no tomorrow."

Myra waited for Rory, but Zeke followed Seth and said softly, "Where they've been, no tomorrow is often the case."

Seth looked guilty. "Sorry, Zeke, that was a thoughtless comment."

"It's okay. I think about the guys we lost from my unit whenever war memories rise up to smack me in the face. My arm injury's nothing compared to guys like Hunter who lost limbs. Or others who lost everything." Zeke's expression sobered even more.

"I didn't mean to remind you of the bad stuff." Seth gripped Zeke's good shoulder and squeezed. "All of that's behind you now. You own a slice of what Hunter calls God's country. Hey, you've never mentioned—uh, do you suffer flashbacks or anything?" Seth lowered his voice as he asked because Myra, Rory and Ghost bustled into the foyer, where the two men still lingered.

The boy and his dog clattered on down the hallway. Myra said, "I thought you two were anxious to get to the dining room."

Smiling, Zeke looped both arms around her. "We were just jaw-boning until you got here. And, Seth, the answer to your last question is no. Myra witnessed one episode that might be classed a flashback. Luckily it came and went fast." He tightened his arms and brushed a kiss over his wife's lips. "Hunter's right in his assessment of Snowy Owl Crossing," he said. "Long winter and all, it's paradise."

Not disagreeing, Seth led the way to the dining room, where the other three men were scarfing down scrambled eggs, cinnamon coffee cake, juice and coffee. "Save us some," Seth entreated. "Has anyone seen Lila? I need to give her the car keys." He dangled them in the air.

Just as he spoke she backed into the dining room through the kitchen's swinging doors, her arms laden with a large bowl of fluffy scrambled eggs topped with crumbled bacon and a steaming pan wafting with heat and the scent of cinnamon. "Did I hear someone ask for me?"

"Me," Seth said to Lila, rushing to take the bowl from her and placing it in the center of the table. "I have the Jeep's keys."

Lila accepted them with a grateful smile. "Thanks. Now sit down everyone. Dig in while it's hot."

Zeke and Myra rounded the table. He pulled out a chair for her before taking his own seat. His friends ribbed him about turning into such a gentleman.

Lila motioned Seth toward an empty chair and handed Myra the fresh coffee cake.

Zeke, who waited to take a slice until Myra served herself, glanced up at Lila. “The Jeep’s fine. How’s your head? Seth said you banged it on the window.”

“What?” Myra stopped dipping out eggs. “Last night you said she was fine.” Her eyes accused Seth before skipping on to Lila.

“No, I didn’t.” Seth helped himself to coffee cake and passed the pan to Ben, who held out his hand. “I believe I said Rory was fine and then explained how Lila came to land in the ditch.”

“Are you all right?” Myra demanded after shooting her brother-in-law a dirty look.

Lila waved a hand. “This morning the spot is only slightly tender to touch. I wish Seth had kept quiet. I didn’t want anyone to know I hit my head hard enough to rattle my teeth. I don’t want my mom to hear. The last thing she said when Tawana and I left the café was to drive carefully.”

“I’m sorry, it slipped out,” Seth explained and patted the empty chair next to his. “Aren’t you going to eat?”

“No. Rory and I ate earlier. In fact…” Pausing, she checked her watch. “I need to run out and feed the horses then load his bike. If I don’t hurry I’ll be late getting him to school. His teacher is a stickler for punctuality. But, you guys…” she said, glancing at Zeke's three friends. "It's been great having you as guests. Safe travels, and do come back when you can stay longer."

Seth shoveled in a bite of egg, took a swig of juice and picked up a second wedge of coffee cake Myra had cut for him. Getting out of his chair, he said to the groomsmen, "You can put your bags in my rental, guys. I'll help Lila." He pulled his keys from his jeans pocket and tossed them to Ben Archer.

"No," Lila protested. "You're a guest."

"One who plans to take a trail ride soon. So far, I haven't had time to ride. As you feed the horses you can give me a rundown on the one least likely to dump me." Seth polished off his coffee cake before he reached the arch. He hesitated briefly until Lila offered a guilty shrug to the others and hurried after him.

"Seriously?" she hissed at Seth as she plucked a jean jacket from the coat tree by the door. "What will everyone think?"

He held the door for her then jogged after her down the porch steps. "What'll they think about what?"

"Mostly Myra and Zeke. I don't want them to get the idea we, uh...well, as a business owner it's not decorous to play favorites among my guests."

Laughing, Seth fell into step beside her. "'Decorous'? What kind of a three-dollar word is that? Are you saying you've never gone to the barn with any other guest?"

Obviously flustered by his question, Lila buried her hands in her jacket pockets and kept her gaze on her boots. "Not one who's male, single and near my age," she mumbled. "Or who is related to my best friend who knows my mom and all of our other friends," she added. "It could be misconstrued."

"There you go spouting big words again," Seth teased, moving ahead of her to slide open the big barn door. "What could be misconstrued?"

"Oh, don't play dumb." Lila took a swipe at his arm, glaring as he deftly avoided her swing. "You're breathing and single, and I'm a youngish widow. In this town if anyone were to mention those two things in the same sentence, rumors would fly. Before you could say Jack Robinson, townsfolk would whisper that we're having a torrid affair."

Seth grinned wolfishly and stopped beside the first stall. "Sounds like something worth exploring. I've never had a torrid affair before. Have you?"

"Stop it. You don't know the people in this town like I do. Last night a couple of the Artsy Ladies poked me about you for no reason other than you're staying here and you were my escort at Myra and Zeke's wedding. They thought they were being funny, but I'm a mother of a boy at an impressionable age, for pity's sake." She flung open a bin of grain and filled a scoop.

Watching her fitful motions sobered Seth. "Point taken. Tell me about the horses," he said, walking with her to the first stall, where a dark horse with a white blaze whickered.

"This is Pendragon. I didn't name them. My husband did. Guiding guests on trail rides was to be his end of the business. After he died, I tried to sell the horses, but money's tight all over." She went back for grain for the second of the four animals, a brown-and-white pinto mare.

"This is Guinevere." She rubbed the mare's silky nose. "The last two geldings are Galahad and Merlin. Kevin loved King Arthur stuff. He planned to name new horses Lancelot and Mordred." Her voice wobbled.

Seth took the scoop and fed the remaining horses, giving her time to gather herself. "Ben wanted us to rent them," he said. "But Gavin didn't think Hunter should risk riding. Not after Zeke told us how Myra got dumped from her horse." Seth set his hand on the neck of the big dappled gray named Galahad. "If they aren't exercised regularly, are they apt to buck?"

Lila shrugged. "Guests have ridden them without problem. I carry extra insurance in case anyone gets hurt. That's mostly why I want to sell them. Are you not a good rider?"

Seth returned the scoop to the grain bin and closed the lid. "I've ridden horses and mules in mountainous terrain leading to some gem sites. It's nothing I've done a lot. But I'd be willing to take them on a few turns around your corral to stretch their legs while I'm here," he said, stopping to close the barn door as they exited.

"That's nice of you."

"No problem. Now, where's Rory's bike?"

"Oh, please, I can get that—I see your passengers gathered at your rental. Rory and I have gotten good at loading and unloading his bike. It's a junior mountain bike, so it fits easily through the Cherokee's hatchback."

"All the same, when you have help available why not take advantage?" He'd no more than finished his suggestion when they saw Rory, weighed down with his backpack, wheeling his bike around the corner of the bed-and-breakfast.

Striding away from Lila, Seth intercepted the boy. "If you open the hatch, I'll toss your bike in and you and your mom can be on your way."

"Uh, okay." Rory ran to the Cherokee. "Thanks," he added after Seth easily slid the bike inside.

"No problem. Have a good day at school." Seth closed the hatch, flung a wave at Lila and crossed over to his friends. "I see Zeke and Myra left," he said, accepting the keys from Ben.

"Yeah. They had chores. Zeke said to call him. He said if this weather holds you can start reroofing the barn soon."

"Lucky you," Gavin said as they all climbed into the SUV. "I mean it," he stressed when the others laughed. "I'd rather be here roofing a barn than returning to Afghanistan."

"How much longer do you and Ben have there? Aren't we bringing all troops home?" Seth asked.

"Not all. I have another sixty days on my assignment," Ben said.

"Three months for me," Gavin admitted. "Who knows after that? I intended to make the army my career, but after coming here..." He stared out his window without finishing.

"I'm only staying until it's time to re-up," Ben said. "Being here made me realize how many places I'd like to see in the U.S. I have a college friend who bought a fishing boat in Alaska. He said anytime I want I can have a job."

"Once the docs fix me up as good as they can, I may come back here," Hunter added. "What about you, Seth? It was hard not to notice the way you leaped up to help Miz Lila. What's her situation? I assume she's divorced?"

Seth screwed his lips to one side. "She's been widowed awhile. But her voice still gets choppy when she mentions her husband. I could be interested, but the few women I've liked enough to get serious have all insinuated I'm a rolling stone. And I don't know what I'd do but hunt for gems."

They left the town behind and their talk turned to travel and other things.

"DID YOU FEED GHOST?" Lila asked Rory after she backed the Cherokee around and headed down the lane. "And did you secure the gate to keep him on our side of the house? We don't need him getting out again like he did last night."

"I pulled on the knob when I saw you and Seth come out of the barn. Did he say anything to you about helping me learn to throw and catch?" Rory asked, leaning forward to stare at his mother.

Her eyes sought his in the rearview mirror. "Helping you…no. Why would he?"

Rory slumped in his seat, clasping his old mitt and

baseball. "I dunno." Then he mumbled, "Zeke said Seth could give me tips on account'a he got awards and trophies playing baseball. He was so good he had scouts looking at him to play for the pros."

"Really? Zeke actually said Seth was that good?"

"Yep. He only told me he played on a city team when he was my age. But I was wishing he'd talk to you about helping me get better."

"Hmm. I'm sorry, honey. He didn't. And unless he does, don't you go bugging a guest, okay? But, gosh, I wonder if he's qualified to teach high school and really coach baseball."

"Huh? Kemper's dad never played ball, but he plays catch with Kemper and teaches him to bat better."

"Well, I heard at the café that the high school coach plans to retire. I think he teaches, too. I just wondered if Seth might be interested."

"Why?"

Lila hid a smile. "Uh, no reason other than probably Zeke would love to have his twin settle in the area." No way would she admit to her son that Seth Maxwell was about the nicest single guy to hit Snowy Owl Crossing in forever.

"I s'pose. If he helped me, I'd like it, too," Rory said.

Chapter Three

Lila stopped at the school and helped her son unload his bike and chain it up. "You have your cell phone? I put it on the charger for you."

Rory opened a small pocket on his backpack and let her see the phone.

"Okay, have a good day. I'll see you at Memaw's café shortly after three."

He closed his pack and dashed up the walkway to catch up to another boy about his height. Lila watched the two horse around then go inside with a gaggle of kids. She waved to a mom pulling into the drop-off circle.

Climbing back into her vehicle, Lila spent a moment missing the kindergarten days when Rory'd wanted a hug and kiss before he skipped into class. They'd gone from that to her giving a quick brush of a stubborn lock of his hair, to a wave, to now nothing but him scurrying away without glancing back. Those milestones signified the passing of time as nothing else could. So many things around her changed, yet she seemed stuck.

On the drive back to the B and B her mind drifted. She'd been a single mom longer than she and Kevin had shared parenting. She wasn't sure why she thought of that now. Other than Seth Maxwell joking this morning about them having a torrid affair.

Lila felt her face heat again. Not only would she not class the sex she'd shared with her husband as torrid, in the five years since his death she hadn't dated.

Thinking back over her marriage, she tried to be honest. She'd been totally green about sex when she'd married at age eighteen. To Kevin, a farm kid, it was a perfunctory part of life. Yes, they'd dated for four years prior to getting married, but dating in Snowy Owl Crossing consisted of sitting together at ball games. Or meeting at the gym for a school dance where, mostly, they stood around. Maybe they held hands at potlucks. That was pretty much it, because kids worked hard in their family businesses. No one had time to hang out idly.

That didn't mean she never had fanciful dreams. Sometimes Kev had fallen asleep, leaving her hot and wanting—wanting to share passionate love with him. But it never happened.

When she arrived back at the ranch that claimed so much of her time and energy, she spared a second to wonder if she'd ever share intimacy with a man sure of himself in the bedroom. Not only sure of himself but caring of her needs, as well.

She parked and went in to clean the now-empty rooms and ready them for the folks scheduled to check in at eleven.

Collecting a stack of clean sheets, she recalled how Seth Maxwell claimed he'd never had a torrid affair. She puzzled over whether she thought that was a lie. Thirty-two, handsome as sin and a world traveler, his saintly declaration didn't fit.

Well, he hadn't claimed to be a saint. And there was a whole lot of space between celibacy and indulging in a torrid affair. But look how fast she'd chastised him for the mere suggestion. Mostly out of habit. Because in a small town rife with gossip she worried about other people's opinion of her. Her best friends pointed out that she cared too much how others judged her. Maybe Seth saw that, too, and had elected to tease her.

But why would he? The sum total of their association had been brief. She stored that thought and called herself silly for presuming to even picture him settling here, let alone the two of them becoming more than passing acquaintances.

Blanking her mind, she hurried on to strip beds and start laundry.

IT WAS 4:00 P.M. when Seth walked into the Snowy Owl Café. It'd been a long round-trip to the Billings Logan International Airport. None of the three guys he'd driven there had been booked on the same flights. For his job, he spent a lot of time sitting in airports, so it hadn't been any big deal for him to wait to be sure none of their flights got canceled, even though they said there was no reason for him to hang around.

The fact was, he had spent too much of his life

booked on Podunk airlines prone to delays and cancellations. He'd forgotten how dependable American carriers were. Dependable schedules, plus nice food courts and gift shops that sold snacks, books, magazines and other stuff in short supply in many foreign airports where he'd twiddled his thumbs. But with all Billings Logan airport offered in the way of food, none of the guys had been hungry after Lila's great breakfast. So here Seth was, well after lunch, and famished as a bear fresh out of hibernation. And there was nary a free seat to be had in the café. He'd never seen the place this full.

Aha! He spotted Zeke and Myra sitting at a table with four burly men—other ranchers, if their faded jeans, plaid shirts and cowboy boots were anything to go by. Cowboy hats hung on the backs of their chairs.

Seth smiled to himself. Cowboy boots was something he'd bought at the airport gift shop. And a hat. The three guys had kidded him, but if he planned to live in the ranch community for a while, he wanted to fit in. The black boots made from buttery leather with a few turquoise cutouts had called to him. Surprisingly they were comfortable. He wondered if Zeke would notice he wasn't wearing his sneakers.

Actually he saw that his brother and new wife were deep in conversation with the folks at their table and four other guys seated at an adjacent one. He wouldn't barge in.

This must be the cattlemen's meeting Zeke had mentioned. Maybe he should just leave and go to Cody's Bar. They served burgers and fries.

He backed toward the entrance, hearing the ding, ding of a bell and a woman yelling, "Order up!" That was when he first noticed Lila taking an order on the far side of the room. She ripped a page from her pad and wove between the tables, headed for the pass-through, where two plates sat beneath a warming light. For a moment she looked straight at Seth, did a double take, stopped and changed course in his direction.

"I only have a minute. Are you here for a meal or to ask me something about the B and B?"

"I stopped to eat, but there's no seating." He jerked a thumb toward the exit. "I figured I'd run down the street to Cody's."

"If you don't mind sharing a small booth with Rory, he's doing homework over in yonder corner." She stabbed her pencil for emphasis.

"Do you think he'll be okay sharing with me? Never mind, I'll go ask him. You have hungry customers."

"Right. And another order to hand in. Mom has a high school student who helps out serving at these big meetings, but she called in sick. It's been crazy." As if to underscore that, Doreen Mercer slapped the bell twice. Orders were waiting.

Lila puffed out a breath and sped off.

Seth made his way to the back booth. His brother looked up and raised a hand in recognition then swiveled in his seat, seeming to check for an empty chair.

Seth shook his head, pointed toward the back and Zeke nodded.

On reaching Rory's booth, Seth said, "Hi, sport. I stopped by to eat, but the place is full up. Your mom suggested maybe I could sit with you."

The boy stopped toying with the fork stuck in a Cobb salad. "Sure." He sat straighter. "Hey, if you want, you can have my dinner. I haven't licked the fork or anything."

Smiling, Seth slid onto the bench seat across from Rory, venturing a guess that the kid disliked lettuce. From the size of the mound left in his bowl, Seth judged the whole of it remained untouched. "It looks good," Seth said. "I may order the same thing. You know, you'll need all of that protein if you're going to play ball."

"Really?" Rory dug his fork under the egg and slices of ham, but kept scowling. "I don't like vegetables, but Mom says I gotta eat 'em."

"You should listen to her. Veggies build strong joints, which you need to swing a bat hard enough to hit a home run."

The kid appeared to still be mulling that over when his mother rushed up, order pad in hand. "Seth, do you need a menu?" She happened to glance down at her son's bowl. "Rory Jenkins, you've hardly taken a bite. Tonight's dessert is your favorite chocolate pudding. But if you don't make a substantial dent in your dinner, you aren't getting sweets. Sorry, Seth." A short sigh escaped her. "What can I bring you?"

"I told Rory that salad looks good. I'll have one, too. And coffee, black."

Lila stood a moment with her pencil poised over

her pad. "Uh, I'll go turn in your order." She gestured toward the kitchen, still not moving, as if she expected him to change his mind.

He flashed a smile. "Great. I'm starved. It'll be a race to the finish to see if Rory beats me to that chocolate pudding."

"You are so full of it," Lila murmured, bending nearer to Seth so only he heard before she whisked away, stopping at a table where four ranchers hailed her.

Satisfaction rippled through Seth when the boy pulled his bowl close to his chest and said, "I'm starting now. I bet I can beat you."

"Hmm, okay, but chew it well so you don't choke."

Seth watched the egg disappear, followed by the cheese. And for perhaps the first time he wondered what he'd be like as a dad. His own father had encouraged and guided him and Zeke, patiently answering scores of sometimes dumb questions. He'd taught them by example, too. Seth couldn't recall a time he'd ever heard his father raise his voice to his boys or their mother, or to anyone at their games as some dads were prone to do. He'd want to be a husband and dad like that.

Stuck on the subject of family, he realized he was almost at the age now that his folks were when they'd had him and his brother. Now that Zeke was married, Seth wondered how long they'd wait to have a kid. Maybe not long. So he'd be an uncle.

Maybe it was time to find his life partner. But, as he'd told Zeke before coming to visit, with his nomadic life the few women he'd found interesting didn't consider him a good long-term prospect.

He couldn't blame them. Sooner or later he always succumbed to the lure of a possible mother lode. It was his career, after all. So was it surprising some women accused him of being more passionate about chasing new gems than he was about them? Spending a minute examining past relationships, he gave an inward wince.

What did that say about him? *What would Lila Jenkins think*?

He cracked the knuckles on his left hand. It was a restless habit.

Rory paused in his eating. "My teacher says not to do that…crack your knuckles. It'll make 'em fat so they won't bend when you get older." The boy's forehead wrinkled. "But you're old and your fingers still bend."

"Hey, I'm not *that* old." Seth laughed, but flexed his fingers several times.

"That's a cool ring," Rory noted. "Is it a snake?"

Seth spread his right hand open on the table. "Yes, I had a silversmith in Italy make it. The snake's eyes are chips from emeralds I found in Thailand."

"Huh. Me 'n Kemper found a snake in his mom's garden once. He had yellow eyes."

Seth shrugged. "I guess I could have had his eyes made from citrine—that's a yellow stone. But I was stoked from finding a nice cache of emeralds that I sold at the Vicenza gem fair."

For a second the boy's expression went totally

blank, then he picked up his fork and began eating again.

Obviously emeralds didn't impress the kid. Seth had encountered that dismissive look before in some adults who learned what he did. Usually not from women who wanted him to give them expensive jewelry. Perhaps that's what he hoped to find in a woman—someone genuinely interested in him, not the gems he unearthed.

Seth saw Lila on her way toward him, juggling what were most probably his empty mug and two coffeepots. As she made her way between tables, she paused to refill cups, including for the table of ranchers who'd waylaid her after she'd taken his order. She had a ready smile that Seth liked. In fact, he found a lot about her to like—very attractive, hardworking, patient, a good mom.

Finally reaching their booth, she set the mug in front of him. "You didn't specify leaded or unleaded. I brought both."

"I'll take regular so I have enough energy to go for a run after I get back to the ranch."

She poured from the pot with the brown top. "Do you run every evening?"

"When I can." He caught her studying his torso. "I'm blessed with good genes. But much of my work requires climbing mountains, which demands that I stay in good shape."

"I know you're a gem hunter. I saw Myra's wedding band. She told us you found the stones, had them cut and set with diamonds. The colored stones are pretty. Blue at times. Purple at others."

"Tanzanite. They're only found in Tanzania and are becoming quite rare."

"Do they just lie around on the ground?" Lila shifted the coffeepots.

Seth laughed. "Most quality gems are dug out of pockets in mountainsides. Rough-cut stones look very different from the finished product you see set in rings or necklaces."

"Oh." The bell announcing an order up dinged a couple of times, causing Lila to turn her head. "Your salad's ready. Would you like a roll and butter with that?"

"No, thanks. I'm probably going to lose the race to Rory. He's been shoveling his in while we've been talking."

Lila shifted her gaze to her son's side of the table and her eyebrows rose in surprise. "He is. Shocking. It's always a battle to get him to eat vegetables, especially green ones. How'd you get him to listen to you?"

Rory answered. "Seth said I need to eat vegetables if I want to hit a home run. And he knows, 'cause don't you remember me telling you Mr. Zeke said Seth got trophies for playing baseball?"

Lila bobbed her head, but before the conversation advanced further she was called away to replenish coffee at another table. She soon scurried back with Seth's salad and was off again.

Seth had decided to let Rory win their eating contest if need be—to help his ego, and so that maybe he'd be happier to eat vegetables in the future. But then wondered if letting a kid win was like throwing a game?

Had his folks ever held back and let him or Zeke come out victorious? He didn't want to think they had. He wanted to think he and his twin had been good enough to win on their own. But he'd definitely ask his dad the next time they spoke. He and Zeke had always had their father as a role model. Who did Rory Jenkins have? It must be hard when a boy only had one parent and she worked two jobs. And Rory seemed as if he understood that his mom was doing her best to make a living.

Rory waved his empty bowl in front of Seth who, himself, was slightly half done.

"I get chocolate pudding before you," the boy crowed.

"So you do. And well deserved. Your mom's swamped. Maybe you should take your bowl and show your grandmother. Isn't she the keeper of the pudding?"

"Yeah." So saying, he slid out of the booth and headed off with his bowl.

Seth had taken another few bites when Zeke walked up. "We're going home," he said. "One of the things that came up during our meeting was that a couple of the larger ranches haven't finished branding their calves yet. Generally they hire extra help, but it seems with our long, harsh winter, not as many cowboys needing part-time work came this far north."

"You're telling me…why? You think I should sign on to brand calves?" Seth's laugh rolled up from his belly.

Zeke laughed, too. "It's not that I don't think you could learn like I did. But late as it is for them to drive their cattle to summer grass pastures, there's no time to train anyone. I'm telling you this because I volunteered to give them a hand the next few days. Which means a delay in roofing my barn. I didn't figure you'd be too bent out of shape. This way you'll get more time to fish. I hear the steelhead are running. Oh, and Lila's mom will buy your catch."

Seth blotted his mouth with his napkin. "I'm not sure I'm keen to fish these swift rivers alone. But Gavin brought up something that snagged my interest. He said before coming here he read up on the area, and some articles said gem hunters have found sapphires near here. Have you heard that?"

"Yep. In fact I told Myra if I mentioned it to you, you'd be sure to visit. Then you phoned to say you'd decided to come and our wedding coincided… Frankly the sapphires slipped my mind." He glanced around the room. "You might want to ask some of the older guys for specifics."

"Cool. I'm no stranger to going online to ferret out information. And a county courthouse will have the facts on what kind of permits are needed and such."

"That'd be in Wolf Point. Not hard to find. It's where Myra and I went for our wedding license. So it sounds as if you're okay having a few days to yourself?"

"I am." Looking past Zeke, Seth saw Rory coming back, carrying a bowl of pudding and wearing a big smile.

"In fact, this morning Lila said her horses needed to be ridden more. I may carve out time to go take a look at the hills beyond here now that I know they may yield some nice gems. Say…how long has Lila lived in Snowy Owl Crossing? Maybe she'll know where sapphires were found. They're probably in defunct mines."

Zeke lowered his voice. "Ixnay on asking Lila, dude," he murmured as Rory approached the booth. "Her husband died in a mining accident." The last bit he imparted half under his breath since the boy noisily plopped down his bowl and spoon and reclaimed his seat.

As Seth tried to digest what Zeke had said, he crushed the napkin he held. Startled by the information about Lila's husband, he quickly decided he'd get particulars on sapphires from another source. He wouldn't want to cause Lila any anxiety.

Myra broke off talking to the couple at another table and signaled Zeke that it was time to go.

"Call or text me after you finish helping your neighbors," Seth said. "In addition to what I said I may do, I may play catch with my little buddy here after he gets out of school."

"Really?" Rory stopped licking pudding off his spoon and his eyes widened. "Really?" he repeated, exhibiting more excitement. "I wanted to ask you, but my mom said no. Oh, but I need a bat. And a mitt that fits," the boy added glumly. "She never has time to shop, 'cause she works so much."

"Equipment isn't a huge deal," Seth told him.

"Gotta take off, bro." Zeke squeezed his twin's shoulder. "Cost for new stuff could turn out to be a big deal. Perhaps you should've spoken with Rory's mom first," he said, a vague warning in his tone. "Pride, you know," Zeke added.

"I will. Go on, get outta here and let me finish my supper or I won't have time to order any of that chocolate pudding before they close the café."

"It was good," Zeke called back with a grin as he moved off and slipped his arm around his wife.

"Will you talk to my mom? She's thinking about signing me up to play on Kemper's Little League team. But she can't seem to decide. Maybe we can't afford it."

Seth registered Rory's downcast demeanor. The poor kid felt let down a lot. But there could be legitimate reasons his mom held back on signing him up to play ball. "How do you do in school?" Seth asked.

Sitting straighter Rory pulled his spoon out of the pudding and stuck it in again. "In school how?"

"In your classes. How are your grades?"

The kid hiked both skinny shoulders and dolefully eyed Seth, who continued to work on finishing his salad.

"I dunno. Mom's not happy if I don't get As on my report card. But Memaw says she got some Bs. Memaw says only Ds and Fs are bad. I never get those."

"Who's Memaw?"

"You know… Memaw." Rory stabbed his finger toward the kitchen just as Lila whipped back to their table carrying the coffeepot.

She gestured with it after topping off Seth's mug. "In Kentucky where my mother grew up, grandparents were called memaw and papaw. I asked her preference when Rory was born. Here people go by grandma and grandpa. But she chose memaw."

Seth grinned. "Whatever makes her happy?"

"Right. I don't know about your mother, but when it comes to guilt trips, mine is the biggest travel agent in the world."

Tipping his head back, Seth laughed long and loud. "Sorry, that description could fit my mother, too."

Lila wagged a finger at her son. "Don't you dare tell Memaw what I said. It's a joke, honey, okay?" Returning her attention to Seth, she grew serious. "It looks as if you're finished. Do you want anything else or just your check? We close in half an hour."

"If that gives me time for chocolate pudding I'll have some. Otherwise I'm good to go. Oh, but something I wanted to discuss with you before I take off… How would you feel about me playing catch with Rory after school? I used to play a lot. I've taught kids in underdeveloped countries. Maybe if you agree, I could give Rory a few batting tips, too."

Rory's eyes widened. "I didn't ask him, Mama. Honestly!"

"No, he didn't ask. Zeke suggested it. And since

my brother is going to help some ranchers and is delaying the roofing, I'll have some free time."

Lila fidgeted. "Rory comes here to do his homework after school. But…it is staying lighter longer. If we get home before dark and you're around, I'm sure he'd love some tips. But I don't want him bugging you," she quickly added when her son did two fist pumps and squealed "Yeesss!" with an ear-to-ear grin.

Seth darted a glance between them. He and Zeke had always had each other to play ball with when no adult was around. "I feel bad that Rory is stuck playing catch with a dog." He said it, but still worried that he might be treading on thin ice with the boy's mom. So it was with hesitation that he broached the next subject. "This morning Zeke and I saw Rory trying to play catch with Ghost. His ball is pretty tattered. And his glove seemed too big. I'll be out tomorrow running errands. Would it be okay if I pick up some equipment more his size?"

Lila's eyes narrowed markedly. Seth steeled himself to be told not only no but hell no from the sparks aimed his way. Funny—it also struck him that her eyes resembled fine, clear, aquamarine stones like those he'd found in Colorado, until hunting them had grown too dangerous due to landslides. But he'd done enough admiring her eyes. Her anger made him wonder if he'd overstepped and ruined everything for the kid.

Then as fast as her temper seemed to flare, her eyes lost their fire. "I know his stuff that I found at a garage sale is old. But I can't afford outlandishly expensive things. Lori Barnes said her husband paid two-hundred-fifty dollars apiece for Kemper's bats. I can't recall what she said mitts cost."

Seth shook his head. "Expensive doesn't necessarily equate to better playing, especially at Rory's age."

"Keeping that in mind, I guess it'll be all right if you buy some new stuff. But only if you promise to give me the bill. I know right now he's anxious to play ball, but who knows if in a month he'll stick with it? I'm just saying he doesn't need equipment with Michael Jordan's name on it or anything."

"Mom!" Rory rolled his eyes. "Michael Jordan played basketball. You mean I don't need a Derek Jeter bat."

Breaking in, Seth said, "Jordan did play pro baseball for a time. He found he liked basketball better. But that's not the point." Glancing at Lila again he said, "I do recommend buying two or three Cal Ripken signature balls. I can probably find them for six bucks or so each. A good, solid ball doesn't get out of round, providing he only lets Ghost play with the old one that's already got teeth marks," he added, turning his attention to Rory again.

Even Lila laughed at that. "I'll go get your pudding," she said, taking off but returning quickly with Seth's dessert.

"Thanks." He smiled at her. "I was afraid it'd be all gone."

"Well, enjoy it, because it's the last one."

Seth didn't dip right in. Instead he followed Lila's

progress to another table, registering that she looked good from every angle. Really good. Then it came flooding back—the tidbit that Zeke had imparted about Lila's husband dying in a mine. Maybe, considering his career, he shouldn't be admiring her. In fact, maybe it wasn't such a good idea to have offered to help Rory. He'd done it mostly because he was a sucker for sad-eyed kids. In the poor countries where he frequently hunted gems, he'd always bring baseballs or soccer balls to hand out to local kids. And he'd give them tips on game rules.

However, Snowy Owl Crossing wasn't a village in a poor country. Seth tried to keep that uppermost in his mind as he polished off the pudding and listened to Rory prattle on about how excited he was to tell his friend Kemper that he got to learn baseball from somebody who had trophies.

Pushing his empty bowl aside, Seth dug out his wallet and peeled off bills enough for his meal and a substantial tip. He dropped the money on the table, stood and said to the boy, "Tell your mother I'm going back to the B and B. Remind her I plan to run. I may take Ghost again. As the only good place to run is along your lane, have her slow down a lot when she leaves the highway." He left the café without checking on Lila's whereabouts.

LILA CAUGHT SETH'S exit from the corner of her eye as she counted out change for Dave Ralston. He was a Cattlemen's Association officer and generally lingered to book a date for their next dinner meeting.

"May we have the last Thursday in June, Lila? Same terms. You close during our business meeting and open to the public after we've all ordered food."

Lila got the calendar on the shelf under the cash register. "Mom hasn't scheduled anything else on that day, Dave. It's yours for the taking." Locating a red marker, she circled the date. "The quilters gather here, but they come after closing. Cattlemen are the only group that's so big you require the whole restaurant."

"I wish we could decide on meeting dates for a whole year at a time, but the ranchers can't all commit so far in advance."

"I know you used to meet at the Grange hall. Mom appreciates the extra business you've brought her since you started coming here."

The leathery-skinned man grinned. "Our guys griped over only getting one kind of meal at the Grange. That's because we hired a camp cook to come in. Now some gripe they can't order a beer with meals here. When's Doreen getting her alcohol license?"

"She's applied. Shall I go ask? She's putting dishes in to wash. Our helper called in sick, which has left Mom and me doing extra duty."

"Nah, don't bother her. She can't get the state liquor board to move any faster. Hank Watson knows someone who sits on that board. I'll ask him to nudge them. G'nite, Lila." As he turned and walked toward the door, he saw Rory crossing the restaurant and he waved to the boy.

"Hey, you've grown a few inches since I saw you

at the Thanksgiving bazaar. Is your mom going to hire you to help around the B and B this summer?"

Rory shook his head. "I'm a kid. I was only nine in April."

"Then I guess you'll enter the junior rodeo at the Wild Horse Stampede."

"Huh?" Rory screwed up his face. "I wanna play Little League baseball. Seth's gonna help me learn to throw good. And bat. He's got baseball trophies. Mr. Zeke said."

"So that's who shared your booth? I thought he looked familiar, but I couldn't place him. Of course I only saw him at Zeke and Myra's wedding."

"Do you know why Seth left before I gave him his check?" Lila questioned her son.

"I brought his money. He left it on the table." Rory scampered to the register and held up the greenbacks.

"Good luck with your ball playing," Dave called and went on out the door.

Accepting the money, Lila counted it and pursed her lips. "Seth left too much. A lot too much," she said. "Even adding in a tip it's still too much." And Lila wasn't sure how she felt about getting a tip from someone who paid to rent from her. She quickly totaled his ticket, put the correct amount in the till and stuck what was leftover in her uniform pocket to return when she next saw Seth.

"Rory, will you lock the door? I'll see if your grandmother needs me in the kitchen for anything."

"I'll sweep," Rory said, tossing the words over his shoulder.

"Bless you. Let me wipe down the tables and get the chairs put up first." She poked her head into the kitchen and spoke to her mom. "Do you need help or should I clean up out here? Rory volunteered to sweep tonight."

"I have the kitchen under control. Could you count out the till? And if you wouldn't mind making a night deposit on your way home, it'll save me walking to the bank. I'll admit I thought it a waste of money when you hired a student to help when we host big meetings. In her absence today it brought home how many steps she saves me. My legs never used to get this tired." Doreen shook her head and wiped her hands on her apron.

Lila stepped fully into the kitchen. "Are you all right, Mom? I don't know when the last time was that I ever heard you complain about anything."

"Like mother, like daughter." Doreen aimed a pointed frown at Lila. "When were you going to tell me about driving your car into a ditch last night?"

"Uh, never. I didn't want you to worry. Who told you?"

"Rory. And by the way, just who is the man who rescued you? How is it that you're letting him buy baseball equipment for Rory? Is he the guy I saw seated with my grandson? He and some other young men came in for lunch a couple of days this week. I thought they were visitors passing through town."

"They were all in Myra's wedding. You were too busy with the reception, I think, to have met them. Three are gone now. Seth Maxwell stayed. He's Zeke's twin and rents from me. He's who sat with Rory tonight. But, Mom, I fully intend to reimburse him for any baseball stuff he purchases."

"Why would he purchase anything?"

"According to what Zeke told Rory, his brother was good enough at baseball to have scouts after him. He's offered to give Rory pointers. Rory's so anxious to play, why not take advantage of his expertise?"

Doreen began pulling pans from the dishwasher and banged them around as she put them away. "I'm not blind, Lila. You spent a good deal of time tonight talking to him. I had to ring more than once to remind you of an order up. All I'm saying is you need to have a care that Rory doesn't come to depend on a man who'll be moving on. Kids, especially fatherless ones, wear their hearts on their sleeves."

"You're thinking about me—about how attached I got to Clay What's-His-Name, that cowboy you dated for two or three years after we moved here."

"Shafer. Clayton Shafer. Hard as it was on me to have him pull up stakes and go work at some ranch in Colorado, it was harder on you. You were ready to call him Dad. When he left, you cried a lot—and blamed me."

"I remember," Lila said slowly. "I'm sorry. Back then I didn't understand that he was a cowboy drifter. I'll keep that in mind now when it comes to Seth Maxwell." Making an X over her heart, she eased out of the kitchen.

But Lila couldn't shake off the exchange she'd had with her mother. An hour later as she drove home and every other sentence out of Rory's motor mouth started with "Seth's gonna teach me..." she honestly didn't have the fortitude to dash his hopes. Learning to play ball so he could join his best friend's team was all Rory wanted at this moment. And she'd had to refuse him things too much in his short life.

She could limit their time together. That's what she'd do. Along with pointing out to her son that Seth was nothing but a coach. A temporary one at that.

Yes, that was a smart plan she decided, driving to the side of the house to park.

"We didn't go in the ditch tonight," Rory announced. "I forgot to tell you Seth might take Ghost for a run and he said you needed to slow down."

"Oh, he did? Well, the house is dark except for the automatic porch light. That means all the guests, including Seth, have retired for the night."

Rory yawned. "I'm sleepy, too."

Inside Lila found Ghost snoring away in the laundry room. So if Seth had taken him for a run earlier, apparently they were both done in.

After tucking Rory into bed, Lila made her nightly visit to the kitchen, where she liked to wind down with tea. She was disappointed not to share Seth's company tonight as they'd done the evening before.

"Whoa, girl," she muttered. "Just...whoa!"

Skipping tea, she went to bed wondering why, when she'd never wasted time mooning over other guests, she could not get Seth Maxwell out of her mind.

Chapter Four

In the morning Lila woke Rory at the usual time. "Your breakfast is ready in the kitchen, buddy. Get dressed and come eat. I'm making quiche for our guests and cutting up fruit for them. Shall I save some apple slices for your lunch?"

"Can I have them with peanut butter?"

"You lost the container we used. Let me see if I have something else."

"I accidentally threw the other one in the trash the day we went on a field trip. 'Cause I didn't take my lunch box, remember?"

"I know. I should have put it in something disposable that day. Listen, don't wear your logo T-shirt again today. Not only is three days in a row too many times for one shirt, but you got chocolate pudding on it last night. Put it in the laundry basket when you feed Ghost. I'll try to start a load before we leave this morning."

"What's a logo?"

"Someone's brand. In this instance, the New York Yankees."

"But that shirt's my favorite, Mom."

"I realize that, but you can't wear a dirty shirt to school."

"O...kay. Will it be clean again by the time we get home this afternoon?"

"Clean, but maybe not dry."

"That's not fair. If I'm not wearing a baseball shirt, Seth could forget he said he'd play catch with me."

Lila wanted to say that given her mother's nudge last night that might be best. But as single-minded as Rory was about baseball, how could she hedge on her support? Their circumstances took a toll on him. Even if keeping a roof over their heads required sacrifices on her part, she hated that it too often negatively impacted Rory's childhood.

"Honey, I'm sure Seth will remember. The shirt goes in the wash," she said and left his room.

Back in the kitchen, Lila quickly gathered ingredients for quiche. But her thoughts lingered on Clayton Shafer. As a kid she'd been a huge daddy's girl. Nothing had been harder than losing him and being forced to move away from her home and her friends. The easygoing cowboy who'd befriended her mom and her the next year had served as a balm to their broken hearts. At the time he came into their lives, Clay Shafer had lived in a bunkhouse on Doug Parson's big ranch. Still, he'd made time to court her mother with candy and flowers. He'd also brought laughter into their lives again.

Handy with tools, Clay had fixed things around the café and in the apartment above, where they lived.

Thinking about it now, she realized he'd also become a fixture in their home. They'd grown to depend on him. By her second year of middle school, she'd taken for granted that Clay was in their lives for good.

Midyear of seventh grade she'd gone home excited to invite him to her first father-daughter banquet. Only seventh graders got to attend and it was a big deal, partly because all the girls got new dresses. Dads bought them corsages. Some of her friends planned to wear their first high heels.

Lila remembered bouncing off the walls waiting for Clay to come by after his workday. He didn't show up. Nor did he come to the café for breakfast. Her mom let her call the bunkhouse to see if he was sick or off moving cattle. When the cowboy who answered the phone said Clayton had received an offer to manage a ranch in Colorado and had packed and left the previous day, the news sent shock waves through her. In truth, like any self-absorbed teen, she'd healed fairly rapidly—thanks in part because Kevin Jenkins, in his quiet way, had begun to notice her.

As she checked on quiche she had in the oven, she wondered if her mom had been scarred by Clay Shafer's callous defection.

Lila got out the cutting board and began chopping fruit. Maybe that was when her mom had changed from carefree to cynical. Certainly she had doubled down on work at the café. Prior to that they'd only been open for breakfast and lunch. After Clay's departure they served food from 6:00 a.m. to 6:00 p.m. Very likely her mom had been the subject of gossip.

Perhaps they both were, and that was why she cared so much what folks thought of her. Why she hadn't flirted or dated since Kevin's death.

Having arranged fruit in a flat container set over ice, Lila carried it to the dining area and placed it on the sideboard. She made sure there were enough plates, silverware and napkins out for her guests.

She heard the door to the laundry room close and barely missed getting mowed over by Rory when he dashed around the corner.

"Yum, something smells good," he said.

"Quiche, which you don't like. I set out your cereal. Say…why are you wearing a jacket?" Lila followed him into the kitchen, where he took a seat at the table.

"I'm cold," he mumbled.

She noticed how he avoided looking at her as he poured his milk. It was a guilty action if ever she'd witnessed one. "Okay, young man, off with the jacket."

"Aw, Mom!"

Bending, she unzipped it and saw what he was hiding—the T-shirt she'd told him to put in the wash. "I cannot believe you deliberately disobeyed me. Hand it over. Now," she said, peeling him out of his jacket.

He crossed his arms and pulled away. "I don't want you seeing me naked."

"Going shirtless until I bring you another is far from being naked." Lila grabbed for the hem just as the oven buzzer sounded and she let go of the shirt.

"I have to take the quiche into the dining room.

You'd better be out of that shirt by the time I return, young man, or else..."

"Or else what?"

"Or else don't even think about playing ball with Seth Maxwell after school."

That threat moved Rory as nothing up to then had. He had the shirt off in a heap on the floor by the time Lila hung up her oven mitts and shut off the oven. Smoldering over his recalcitrance, she scooped up the offending shirt and bolted from the room only to run smack into the man who'd played a part in this latest dispute.

SETH TEETERED ON the slant heels of his new boots. He grabbed her upper arms to keep them both upright. "Hey, hey. Slow down. I was coming to find you to let you know I fed the horses. Last night your other guests mentioned riding to the river this morning. If you like, I can help them saddle up. And one of the women asked if I knew which horses were the gentlest."

Lila sucked in a deep breath and let it out. "Why would you feed my horses? And why would I expect you to help the others? You, too, are a guest."

Seth released her and frowned into her upturned face. "You have a packed schedule. I'll be here a few more weeks at least, and yesterday you said you didn't have time to look after the stock properly. I thought—wait, you look mad. Have I done something to cause that?"

"Only roundabout," she said, dangling Rory's T-shirt

by a sleeve. "I let him buy this New York Yankee shirt at the start of school. He wants to wear it all the time. This morning I insisted he put it in the wash. Instead he came to breakfast hiding it beneath his jacket. His reason for rebelling is that he's afraid if you didn't see the logo, you'd forget promising to play catch with him. I know that may sound to you like a silly reason for me to be steamed, but his blind focus on baseball is getting to be too much."

"I follow through on my offers, Lila. Will you tell him that?"

She nodded. "I hate how often I've had to disappoint him."

"It's evident you're a lady with a lot on your plate. Which is why I want to help since I'm kicking back here until Zeke roofs his barn. That's delayed because he's pitching in to brand calves for neighbors. How is my helping you different?"

"Zeke is a rancher now, and neighbors will help him if need be. You're my paying guest. I could reduce your rent, but it was a long winter with no renters."

"You are one stubborn woman," Seth said even as he tucked an errant curl behind her ear.

Lila broke out in a grin. "So I'm told. 'Hardheaded' is how Mom puts it. Okay, I'll give in gracefully. And, thanks. Now I have to make sure this goes in the wash, and take Rory a clean shirt. We're running late. I did plan to turn the horses into the grassy corral. If you'll do that and help the others saddle up, next time you're at the café I'll buy your supper. Which reminds me, last night you left too much money for your meal."

"I always tip well. Assures future good service." He held up both hands when she puffed up again. "We'll argue about the tip later." He turned aside. "Hey, you never said which horses will be best for the ladies."

"Guinevere and probably Merlin. Both have good dispositions."

"Got it. I'm ready to help myself to breakfast. Something smells so good it's making my mouth water."

Lila had headed down the hall, but glanced back. "I hope you believe real men eat quiche. The ranchers scoff, so Mom can't put it on the café menu. Instead she bakes the same thing in a deep pan without crust and calls it cowboy frittata."

"Too funny."

Laughing, Seth served himself a double slice of the quiche that had spinach, mushroom, crumbled bacon and onion. He ate it and some cantaloupe and pineapple then poured a to-go mug of coffee to take to the barn. He heard the washer go on, but since Lila hadn't returned with another shirt for Rory, he left. He got a kick out of sparring with her, but wasn't above calling it quits while they were even.

He had turned the last of the four horses into the grassy corral by the time Lila drove off. Rory saw him and waved. Seth waved back.

It wasn't long before the two couples staying at the B and B came out. One of the men hailed Seth and jogged up to the fence. "I know we were asking about the horses, but we're gonna drive to the river to fish. Lila said her mom wants to buy any fish we catch to serve at the café, so we need to take a cooler. We'll ride to the lake tomorrow and take a picnic lunch. You're welcome to join us to fish today."

"Thanks, but I have errands to run. Tomorrow, I'll help you saddle up."

"That's not necessary. Let me apologize for assuming you worked here. Lila informed us this morning that you're a guest."

"No apology necessary. I came for my brother's wedding, and they're all good friends. I'm staying on awhile and I want to pitch in. Makes me feel useful rather than decorative." They all laughed then parted after agreeing Seth would help ready the horses if he was out and about the next morning.

The couples drove out and Seth went upstairs to shower. Before he headed to town he took a final turn around the dining room, again thinking with all Lila did she was amazing. But it was mind-boggling to see how she gave guests free rein of her house. He knew her private quarters were locked because it said so on a card taped to the back of his room door, along with a request to treat the Owls Nest as if it "was your own home." That bothered him some. However, it was her house. Only there was something making him want to look out for her.

Shaking off the feeling, he made sure he had his front-door key before he locked up. First item on his to-do list was to find the county library.

A phone app directed him to an adjacent town where Zeke said he'd also find the courthouse. He drove past a sporting-goods store on his way to the library. That meant he'd be able to take care of all his errands without running all over creation.

At the library he hunted up a librarian rather than poke around on his own. "Hi," he said to a woman pushing a book cart. "I'm interested in locating any material you may have relating to sapphire finds in the area."

The gray-haired lady studied him through wire-rimmed glasses. "I've lived here all my life. I only know of two such reports. Most Montana gemstones are found in abandoned gold and copper mines in the state's heartland. Here we're mostly about cattle and fishing. So if you came here to strike it rich, you may be wasting your time."

"I'm here visiting family, but gem hunting is my trade. A friend said he'd read that sapphires were found near Snowy Owl Crossing. I'd like to check it out."

"If it's your trade I guess you know abandoned mines can be treacherous. Even though they're closed, you'd be required to have a permit to excavate in them."

"I'm aware of that."

"Come, I'll show you the newspaper archives. We're in the process of having back issues digitized, but our crew is nowhere near working on the dates you'll want. The copper in the Rainbow Mine played out eight years ago. Some guys took clear quartz out of it last year. Opportunity Mine ran three shifts hauling gold and copper. It's been maybe five years since they suffered a terrible tunnel collapse. Upper runs caved in on a lower cut they were digging. Eighteen miners died. There was talk of lawsuits, but the state mine board ruled it an accident. Tragic all the same for some local families."

Seth murmured an agreement, wondering if that was where Lila's husband had worked.

"Opportunity Mine was where a couple of brave or stupid men claimed to have found a dozen sapphires. They went back a second day, but came out swearing they'd heard ghosts or some such tripe. They cleared out of town. Far as I know, the stories kept other hunters away."

"Interesting. I'm no stranger to evil-spirit legends. Superstitions are entwined with gems, especially in Asia and South America." Seth smiled. "In some areas it's hard to hire guides. I haven't made definite plans to search here. If I do, I'll be careful."

The woman stopped in the back corner of the library and tapped the face of a few file cabinets. "The month and years filed in each drawer are listed on the front."

"Thanks." Seth pulled a small note pad and pen out of his shirt pocket.

"Good luck," she said and left him to his own devices.

He found an article on the Rainbow Mine first. As the librarian noted, a crew reported digging there the summer after the mine closed. They'd found clear quartz and some smoky crystals. Apparently not enough to bring the hunters back. Seth knew clear quartz sold for more now than it used to, but not enough to waste his time.

He next located a series of articles on the pair who'd found sapphires in the mine named Opportunity. Reporters had chosen to write human-interest pieces that tied their experiences to a haunted mine. One suggested perhaps poison gases in the old tunnel had made the gem hunters dream up ghosts.

Seth went back to the drawer that held papers printed the year of the mine accident. It took longer, but he finally located issues where it had made headline news. He found Kevin Jenkins among the names of missing miners. That must be Lila's husband. He didn't see a specific story about her and Rory, but the articles were still sad. He considered not writing down who currently owned the Opportunity Mine. However, if only two gem hunters had taken out a few high-grade sapphires, likely there were more. And that mine actually sat quite near Zeke and Myra's ranch.

Seth took a break, sobered by the tragedy that had taken the life of someone dear to people he had come to like a lot. Would any gems he might find be worth possibly raking up bad memories for Lila? On the other hand, he could do some initial exploration without explaining anything to her. After all, she hadn't expressed an interest in what he did for a living.

Pocketing his notes, he thanked the librarian. Rather than go directly to seek information on permits, he elected to stop at the sporting-goods store.

He initially picked out a youth mitt and several baseballs. He stood in an aisle testing bats when a passing clerk said, "You must have a son or daughter starting Little League next week."

"No. These are for a friend." The man's casual comment pricked Seth's conscience, causing him to again ponder what it'd be like to have a child to guide in ball playing and other activities. He pictured a baby he'd watch grow. For that to happen he'd have to set down roots. He grimaced, thinking of two of his serious girlfriends. Both were married with families now.

The clerk continued to hover. "Do you want the high-end bats that some parents are buying?"

"Not at the moment. This boy's mother asked me to stick to a budget." He added two adult mitts to his stack. "Can I leave these at the counter while I check out backpack oxygen tanks and masks?"

"Sure. If you're planning to dive in any of our lakes, you'll need a wetsuit."

Seth shook his head. "Not necessary." Reluctant to admit he might be descending into an abandoned mine, he ignored the clerk's obvious interest. He owned top-of-the-line equipment he had stored with a friend in Italy who, since he'd married, had given up gem hunting. Trailing the clerk to where masks and packs were displayed, Seth spared a minute to wonder why, when women loved gems, they'd be dead set against the process it took to find and bring them to the earth's surface. He quickly counted the number of buddies he'd lost to love and marriage. More than a few needled him about letting love pass him by. All seemed perfectly happy working other jobs.

He wouldn't mind finding someone special, but what else did he know? His college degree was in geology, but most of those jobs required travel, too.

Finding the right aisle, he focused on the small display. He picked up a mask, put it down and dusted off one that came with a headlamp. If the same clerk checked him out, that item would be a dead give-away as to his intention. Although caving would be another sport requiring this gear, he had no idea if any caves, charted or uncharted, existed here. The minute he decided to buy this stuff, he realized on some level he'd already hoped to have a look-see at Opportunity Mine.

He added the mask with the lamp to his purchases. Next he'd go to the courthouse to apply for a permit. It was always possible he couldn't get one. Maybe he ought to wait to buy the equipment. But it was too late; a clerk had started to ring him through. The older man at the register didn't question why Seth wanted a separate check for the ball gear. He thought he'd better have it because he was sure Lila would insist on reimbursing him.

At the courthouse a short time later, a clerk told him the Rainbow Mine was in receivership. The Op-portunity Mine had become property of the state, which sometimes happened when mining went bad. If a mine no longer produced, no company wanted to pay property taxes on useless land.

"Thanks for the information," he told the helpful clerk. "I'll fill out a permit request to explore the mine owned by the state. Any idea how long it may take to get through the system?"

"I'll fax it to the department in Helena. Summer has higher demand for permits. It's still early, though. You could hear back in three weeks or so. You'll get a letter that'll include a permit or a rejection. If rejected, they'll tell you why."

"Three weeks works. I haven't decided how long to stay and visit my family, but I'll be here that long for sure." Because he'd arranged with Zeke prior to his visit to receive his mail at the ranch, he wrote their address on his permit request. Doing so made him feel a little guilty, as if he were hiding something from Lila. Again he reminded himself that dealing in finding and selling expensive gemstones was how he made his living.

Semisatisfied with his day trip, he elected to look at the ball field where Lila said League games were played. He climbed from his vehicle to survey the park. It looked like every other small ball field. Open bleachers. Worn tracks to the bases. A bent mesh fence behind the catcher. Perimeter lights for night games. All suitable for nine- to twelve-year-old kids.

Next he stopped for a late lunch at an Old West restaurant boasting a lot of cars in its parking lot.

While eating a steak burger, Seth wished he could think of a gift for Lila. He was reasonably sure she didn't currently have an important man in her life. But he didn't know that for certain.

He considered buying her flowers and recalled

seeing a flower nursery on the outskirts of town. Although maybe cut flowers were too intimate. He could buy a potted plant. But would she see that as making more work for her to remember to water it?

After lunch, he pulled into the nursery—just to look around.

"May I help you?" a woman called. She stood at a table arranging cut flowers in crystal vases.

"Is it okay if I browse? I'm not sure what I want yet."

"Wander to your heart's content. I'm making arrangements for a wedding reception. I'll be here if you have questions or find something."

Seth strolled aimlessly among pots. He paused at a table of violets and remembered in Boston his mother had a row of different kinds on her kitchen windowsill. He thought Lila had salt and pepper shakers on hers.

Beyond the violets he spotted blooming rosebushes. He could picture one on Lila's porch bringing color and welcome to her and her guests. He liked red, but then spotted a bush with a profusion of salmon-colored buds. They would look really nice against the weathered-gray siding of the house. The container, too, was made of wood. Beautiful but not too fancy. Pleased with his decision, Seth picked up the rosebush and carried it to the front of the store.

"Ah, you found something." The flower lady dusted her hands on her apron and motioned to the counter where there sat an old-style cash register. "A very nice choice," she said, peeling the price off the bottom of the wood. "Would you like me to tie a satin bow this same shade around the pot?" she asked.

"Thanks, but I'll take it as it is," Seth told her and handed over his credit card. "It's not for any special occasion. I just think it'll look nice by the front door."

"The roses have only recently come out of our hothouse. We shouldn't have another freeze this late in the spring. But one never knows. If the weather turns, set the pot inside and you'll be all right." She smiled as she rang up his purchase and gave him the sales slip to sign.

The first thing he did after parking in his usual spot beside the bed-and-breakfast was to set the rose next to Lila's front door. He descended the steps again and admired it. The bush looked exactly as he'd imagined, inviting and colorful.

He checked his watch and saw he'd wiled away most of the day. Even if Lila left the café shortly after it closed, he still had a good hour or more before she and Rory got home.

Going to his room, he changed out of his slacks and boots and into jeans and sneakers. He had plenty of time to take Ghost for a run and still tape the handle of the wooden bat he'd bought Rory.

SOME FORTY MINUTES LATER, he was sitting on the top porch step taping the bat handle to ensure a better grip, when Lila drove in. The other guests had stopped by, bubbled over with news of the fish they'd caught and how delighted Doreen Mercer had been to get them. The women in the foursome admired the rosebush. Seth had smiled at their delight and also chuckled because neither of their husbands had noticed the potted plant.

Rory didn't, either. He zeroed in on the bat in Seth's hand and the ball in a mitt on the porch. "Oh, wow. Oh, wow," the boy shouted, running up the few steps to shed his backpack and plop down next to Seth.

"Are these mine?" he asked, his eyes huge and his freckles standing out against his pale face.

"They are. And it's still light enough for us to try them out," Seth said, glancing at Lila, who moved at a much slower pace toward the steps.

"Kemper has green bats," Rory announced, touching the sleek, dark wood of the bat Seth had taped and was now tearing off the excess and smoothing the edges down.

"This one is made of solid hickory," Seth said. "It meets all League regulations. Some pro ball players still prefer wooden bats."

Lila had reached the steps. She shifted her purse to the other shoulder and seemed to take in everything before stepping up. "Oh…oh…that rose is beautiful. Where did it come from?"

"I passed a nursery after I left the sporting-goods store. The rose called to me," Seth said, deliberately making light of the agony he'd gone through to choose it.

"It's perfect there," she said, her eyes shining with tears. "I don't know why I never thought to buy something to decorate the porch. It's the very touch needed to greet guests. I've no idea what it cost, Seth, but you must let me reimburse you for the rose and Rory's equipment."

"The rose is a gift." Seth's tone brooked no argument on that score. "Hey, why don't you change into jeans and come toss the ball around with us until it gets dark?"

"I, uh, c-couldn't," Lila sputtered. "I need to cut out baby layettes—that's my project for my women's group to sell at the next bazaar. We're raising money for a snowy owl refuge."

"At most we have an hour of light." Seth pulled two adult mitts out of the sack tucked behind the porch railing. "I took the liberty of buying you a glove."

"Please, Mom." Rory begged her with his eyes, too. "You used to play with me, or read, or do puzzles. You never do anything now 'cept work."

Seth knew the moment she capitulated. Her smile slipped and her shoulders bowed. "I, uh…let me feed Ghost and change. You guys start without me."

"I took Ghost for a run and I fed him," Seth said. "He could come out, but maybe we should break in this new ball first. Another day we can show Ghost he only gets to chew on Rory's ratty old baseball."

"Sure. Thanks for feeding him," Lila said, bending to sniff a rosebud. She slanted a happy smile at Seth that had his heart beating faster before she went inside.

"Come on, Seth. I can't wait," Rory shouted, all but hopping up and down when Seth handed him a blue leather outfielder youth glove. "This is cool.

Cooler than Kemper's brown glove. After we practice, if Mom lets me, I'm gonna phone him."

Seth left the smaller of the two adult gloves on the porch for Lila. He put on the larger one and massaged the new ball a few times. "Let's leave batting practice for another day. Tonight we'll get the feel of throwing and catching a ball."

Nodding vigorously, the boy ran to the side of the house where Seth had first seen him tossing his old ball in the air. Rory turned to face him and Seth gave an easy toss. The ball bounced in and out of Rory's new glove and hit his head.

"I missed it," he said ruefully as he rubbed his forehead.

"Let the ball come down to your level instead of reaching for it," Seth instructed. "It'll take time to get used to the new glove. Gently squeeze the ball the instant you feel it touch the mitt. Cover it with your free hand so the ball stays firmly in the pocket."

"Nobody told me that before." Rory threw the ball to Seth.

It went wild and he had to dive for it. Then he took a minute to show Rory the right way to throw from his shoulder, not his elbow.

The boy said, "This is good. At recess no one wants me on their team 'cause they say I throw like a girl."

"That's not nice," Lila said, letting the door slam as she emerged from the house. She scooped up the spare mitt and made her way to them. "Tell your friends some girls throw better than boys, and they can run faster, too."

"She's spot-on," Seth declared and tossed her the ball, which she caught neatly.

Lila gave Rory a soft toss, which he held on to. The success had him dancing excitedly.

Following a few more good catches, Seth noticed Lila relaxing and smiling a lot. And she looked darned appealing in snug jeans and a T-shirt. A thought he savored more and more as they continued to play even after the sun dipped low and evening shadows threatened to end their outdoor time.

Lila, though, acknowledged the fading light. "Hey, guys, as much fun as we're having, we almost lost that last ball in the dark. Time to call it a night."

"Aw, Mom. I'm really getting the hang of closing my mitt around the ball like Seth showed me. Can we throw a few more? Please, please, please?"

She shrugged. "Two more rounds then we're done."

Rory threw to Seth. He had to back into a row of bushes to catch the ball. He tossed underhand from that distance to Lila.

Seemingly out of nowhere swooped a giant bird directly over Seth's head. He ducked and cringed as the flapping bird skimmed his hair to catch the ball in its talons.

Then the thief flew off with his prize.

Rory jumped around bawling and bellowing, "Stop. Stop him. That bad owl took my brand-new ball." His screech ended in copious tears.

Lila, who'd dropped to her knees to escape the

snowy owl's path, reacted to her son's howl. Leaping up, she ran to his side and gathered him against her.

Coming closer, Seth circled both of them in his arms, one hand cupping the back of Lila's head. "Rory," he said calmly, "I bought three balls. Don't cry. Think about the story you'll have to tell at school tomorrow. That was awesome."

Clutching at Seth, Lila concurred. "Right, Rory. Do you remember Auntie Myra telling us how an owl tried to fly off with Orion? Tomorrow we'll laugh when we think how upset the bird will be to discover the leather he stole isn't covering anything good to eat."

The boy dried his eyes on Seth's shirt. "It'll serve him right." He snuffled. "Auntie Jewell told my class one time that snowy owls mostly hunt food out in the fields. I'll pay you back for the ball, Seth."

Lila ruffled the boy's shaggy hair. "I'll do that. Now, though, I want to go in and call Jewell—she thought all the owls left the area. Thank Seth for playing catch and buying new stuff." Lila deftly untangled them.

"Thanks, Seth." Rory moved toward the house with his mother. "Can we play again tomorrow?"

Lila shushed him. "Didn't I tell you not to bug Seth? If he has time he'll tell you."

Missing the feel of holding them, Seth followed a pace behind. "It takes regular practice to get good at any sport. But, Lila, I know you don't always get to leave work as early as you did tonight. Isn't there a park down the street from the café? I'd be glad to meet Rory there to practice. Maybe that'll save us from losing balls to owls," he said, scanning the darkening sky over his shoulder. "Or from having Ghost out using them as chew toys," he added.

Lila laughed. "How can we turn down an offer like that? But I mean it, Seth, if you have other fish to fry, tell Rory no."

"Memaw's gonna fry fish tomorrow at the café. Why is Seth frying some?"

Seth held back a snicker and let Lila explain the saying was another like "right as rain," which she'd used the other day. After entering the foyer they went separate ways.

Seth climbed the stairs to his room, thinking he didn't know when he'd enjoyed himself more. In spite of the owl incident, tonight had a hominess to it he hadn't fully realized he'd missed until he'd experienced it. It had been a long, long time since anyplace he'd landed truly felt like home. And Lila—well, he couldn't go there yet, but he owed Zeke and Myra for booking him into the Owl's Nest.

Chapter Five

Lila's arms still tingled from the friction of Seth's big hands rubbing away her goose bumps. She'd never heard of a snowy owl attacking a human, but having one snatch something as she reached for it left her heart thundering all the same. Yet if she was honest she'd admit the second kick of the organ happened after the owl had flown away. Her heart sped markedly after Seth got all protective and cradled her and Rory with his solid body. And it had felt nice.

"Mom, can I take my glove and new bat to school tomorrow? I want to show them to Kemper. And I'll have them if Seth comes by the café when school's out."

Her son's request interrupted Lila's musings. "How about if we put your name on the mitt and on one of the baseballs to show they're yours? You'll be riding your bike from school to the café. Carrying a bat might be too awkward."

"Yeah. I wish I had two bats. I could leave one at Memaw's. Kemper has three."

"Young man, you're lucky to have one. Nothing good comes from being greedy."

"But I thought you said we can always make wishes."

Surprise flowed happily through Lila, knowing her son had not only listened to her but had apparently grown up enough to digest some of what she'd said. "It doesn't hurt to wish. How about you shower and hop into bed? I'm going to phone Jewell. I'll come shut out your light when she and I finish talking."

"Okay, but I wanted to call Kemper to tell him about my baseball stuff."

"I left my phone in the kitchen. I'll go get it and bring it to you. It's a school night, though. So you can't talk long."

"Yay. I only wanna tell him about my new mitt and how I'm catching better with it. I am, aren't I, Mom?"

"Definitely. I saw that in the short time we played catch."

He ran off to his bedroom. Lila couldn't tame her smile. She loved seeing him so happy. What she was less sure about—how much that joy depended on Seth, a guest they all knew was very likely just passing through.

In the kitchen, she set a mug of water in the microwave for tea before she picked up her cell phone. It surprised her to see she'd missed three calls. All were from Jewell. Rarely was anything important enough going on among the Artsy Ladies to warrant so many attempts to reach her.

The microwave dinged. She dipped a tea bag several times in the hot water, then shut out the light and carried the mug and her phone back to her bedroom. With guests who could arrive home any minute and stop by the kitchen, Lila wanted to make the personal phone call in private.

Kicking off her shoes as she sat on the bed, she heard the upstairs shower connected to Seth's room go off. Savoring a sip of tea, she brought up Jewell's number.

"Hi, it's Lila. What's up?"

"Tawana's in the hospital. I ran into Eddie Four Bear at Ralston's ranch. He said she had a severe gall bladder attack. Apparently it's not her first. She went to the reservation clinic and the doctor sent her to the hospital for surgery tomorrow."

"That's awful."

"Yes."

"Weren't you two going to Washington, DC, soon?"

"Heavens, I may have to go alone," Jewell murmured. "I'm trying to get my scheduled appointments caught up first. I know how busy you are, Lila, but do you think you'd have time to visit Tawana and take her flowers from our group? Myra's pickup is in the shop and Zeke is helping a neighbor brand calves all week. Shelley is firing ceramics and can't leave her kiln. Mindy still hasn't bought a car."

"Sure, I'll figure something out. Seth Maxwell suggested helping Rory practice ball after school tomorrow… I can ask if he'll bring Rory home so I can visit Tawana. How long will she be in the hospital?"

"I'm not sure. Like I said, she's had other attacks. You know she never complains. The MRI didn't look good was all Eddie said—Seth Maxwell is playing ball with Rory?"

"Yeah, he picked up some baseball equipment for Rory today. We all played catch tonight, which is why I missed your calls."

"Oh, really? How come Seth got Rory baseball equipment? Are you two getting cozy?"

Lila thought about how she'd felt having Seth's strong arms around her. Cozy came to mind. But that reminded her why she'd intended to call Jewell, even before seeing the missed calls. "Zeke mentioned Seth played a lot of baseball growing up. According to Zeke, their family thought Seth might make a career of baseball. Lord knows Rory needs practice if he has any hope of joining Kemper's team. That's a short version."

"Wow!"

"I actually planned to phone you tonight, anyway. While we were playing catch, a snowy owl swooped down and made off with one of Rory's new baseballs. You should've seen it. The bird plucked it right out of the air. Did you know some of the owls stayed here?"

"Yes, two pair at least. Zeke said the guys saw a male carry off a rat near where you put your SUV in the ditch. I rode out to Leland's timber this morning and took photos. One of the four is a bird I'd banded. The fact they didn't all migrate validates our urgency to secure a preserve. I sure hope that's what the committee concludes."

"Good luck. Are you traveling there, presenting and coming straight back?"

Jewell stammered a bit. "N-not really. I have a couple of other errands planned. Pete Cooper is covering my practice in case you need a vet for any of your animals."

"Okay. What a great place to sightsee. I'd love to take Rory to all the museums and memorials. Bring back pictures to share."

Jewell remained silent another moment. "Uh, don't count on that, Lila. I'm driving to a stud farm in Maryland in my free time. Mark Watson wants to raise a different type of saddle horse. There's a part-Morgan sire on a farm there he's asked me to see and, if he checks out, buy sperm."

"No kidding? That's like work. Jewell, you can't go to DC and not take any time for yourself."

"You're wringing this out of me, Lila. And if you share this with another soul I'll be upset with you forever."

"Don't you know me better by now? I'm no gossip."

"I know, but I'm all muddled. Last week Leland asked me to stop by. When I did, he said Saxon has a concert not far from the horse farm where I'll be. I checked. They're close. It shocked me that Leland mentioned Saxon. He never has before. Then I wondered if, like your mom said, maybe he's more ill than we know. Otherwise why would he give me a ticket to Saxon's concert and ask me to deliver a letter? He wants Saxon to come for a visit. He must want reconciliation. Not sure how that'll sit with Saxon. Those two never bonded."

"Ouch! Jewell, are you sure you want to put yourself in the middle of their conflict? I mean everyone thought you and Saxon—uh, it's none of my business. Just don't let him break your heart again."

"What makes you think he broke my heart?"

"Come on, Jewell."

"I gave him up because he couldn't really stay in Snowy Owl Crossing. I thought I'd hidden my true feelings. I meant for everyone to think he and I simply went our separate ways after college."

"More like we all felt you were too hurt for us to ask what had happened."

"I had no idea. Honestly, Lila, I loved him once. I'm not sure I'm strong enough yet to contact him. I did look online and this concert in Maryland is one of many. As big a deal as he's become in country music, he probably has handlers who keep his crazy fans at bay. But maybe I can give one of them Leland's letter."

"Is that what happened? Did he get too friendly with fans?"

"Nothing like that. Our falling-out really was more my fault than his."

"Well, what I do know—what all your friends would swear to—is that without your encouragement when Saxon was in junior high and high school, he'd never have begun to play guitar, let alone write or sing songs. Did he get too big for his britches?"

"No. Maybe. I don't know. He needed to be in Nashville. From the time I saved my first injured animal I was bent on being a vet in Snowy Owl Crossing. If you ever fall in love again, don't give the man you love an ultimatum, Lila. It's devastating if he doesn't choose you."

"So true. I tried that with Kevin over mining. Had he listened to me I wouldn't be a widow and Rory would have his dad. I should have insisted he not go into the mines regardless of how much money they paid. Thankfully I'll never have to choose again. But don't assume Saxon was right to be pigheaded. Maybe he was selfish."

"No, but you're good for my ego. Thanks for the pep talk. Hey, tell Tawana I'll call her from DC. And, Lila, please don't share our discussion with anyone. When Saxon and I split, I couldn't bear being the talk of the town. The thought still makes me shudder. I may yet hand my concert ticket to a stranger on the street and ask them to deliver Leland's letter."

"Cross my heart I won't breathe a word. Do what you can to get us an owl habitat." Lila heard Jewell mumble goodbye.

For a moment she sat holding her phone, replaying the personal parts of their conversation. It didn't surprise her to hear Jewell all but admit she'd loved Saxon Conrad—and maybe still did. Love was so unpredictable. The why, the how, the who anyone chose to love could be painful.

Sparing a deep sigh for her good friend, Lila slowly climbed off her bed. She took her phone to Rory's bedroom. Apparently she'd talked too long. He had fallen asleep. She felt guilty, but he could call his friend in the morning.

Rory lay on his side with his cheek on his new ball mitt. She leaned down and tenderly touched his mussed, damp hair before easing the mitt away so its laces wouldn't leave grooves on his face. He stirred but didn't wake.

Lila set the prized mitt on his side table then exited the room, reaching back in to shut off his light. She returned to her bedroom, remembering what her mother had said a few months ago: that Rory would flit from wanting to play baseball to soccer, or if he shot up another foot, to basketball. Yet his allegiance to baseball hadn't wavered.

Because she operated from sticky notes, Lila jotted herself a reminder to buy Tawana flowers, which cued her to picture the lovely rosebush Seth had bought her. No one had ever given her gifts for no reason. In her slice of the world even gifts for birthdays or Christmas tended to be practical. Flowers were reserved for funerals or hospital stays.

So why did one beautiful, blooming rosebush give her shivers of pleasure? Lila didn't want to dwell on it. It made no sense that a single guest at her B and B could waltz in and in short order make her feel fuzzy headed. She'd rented out rooms since before Rory was born. This was the first time in memory that she daydreamed about a guest and in so doing felt young again and giddy.

Fortunately she heard her two other sets of renters enter the house. They laughed together and went into the kitchen and back out, then climbed the stairs. Their trip to the kitchen reminded Lila they'd left her a note on her chalkboard asking her to fix them a picnic lunch tomorrow. It was a service she enjoyed providing. She'd never gone on a picnic, but had a romantic view of them and so wrote that on her to-do list. Then she set her alarm for an hour earlier than normal so she could bake cookies.

IN THE MORNING Seth swung open the kitchen door and nearly hit Lila, who had omelets and sausage patties on a tray to take into the dining room for guest breakfasts.

"Sorry," he said, steadying her. "I came to ask if it'd be okay to take Ghost out to the barn while I feed the horses."

Her cell phone played a tune, stopping her from immediately answering. Rather, she shoved the tray of plates against his chest. "Can you put these under the warming lights so I can see who's calling me so early?"

"Sure." He took the tray and crossed the room to unload it, but paused as he heard Lila shriek.

"Mom, talk slower! How did you fall?"

Seth quickly set down the tray and returned to stand near Lila. Her brow furrowed, she put up a hand as if attempting to rub the wrinkles away.

"But you are mobile, right? Can you call Arnie Fitzwater? Either he or his son will drive you if they aren't out on a tow job. Rory's still in bed. I need to get him up and fed before school."

Lila stopped talking, listened and then said, "Mom, if you have no feeling in your fingers and arm, and there is pain in your neck and shoulder, you need to see a doctor. I know… I'm a fine one to talk. I can come take you to the clinic, but who will open the café for breakfast?" Her troubled gaze met Seth's. "I don't know what we'll do tomorrow. Let's get through today."

Seth dug car keys out of his pocket and dangled them in front of Lila's eyes. "I'll go take her to Emergency. You handle what needs doing here."

"I'm in the kitchen making picnic lunches for a group going on a trail ride today. You hear Seth Maxwell. He stopped to say he'd feed the horses. Now he's offering to drive you. Just let him, Mom. Maybe he'll wait there and bring you back to the café. Then we'll decided what to do next."

Seth gave Lila an awkward one-armed hug and she hugged him back. He didn't wait to hear more of the conversation. He already knew Lila's mother had reservations about him, although he wasn't sure why. Maybe if the two of them were confined in his car she'd tell him.

TRAFFIC WAS NONEXISTENT. In less than fifteen minutes Seth knocked at the café door. It surprised him to have Doreen open right up and step out. Her right arm was pressed tight to her chest. With her left, she fumbled a jacket, purse and a ring of keys.

"Here, let me help." Seth draped the jacket around her shoulders and took the keys. "Okay, the door is locked. Let me help you into the car." Doreen grimaced when Seth got in on his side and fastened her seat belt.

"I missed hearing how this happened. Do you think your arm is broken?"

"Coming out of the walk-in cooler, I slipped on a spot of water. I went down like a rock and hit my elbow on the tiled floor. Of course, I'm right-handed." She fretted. "I can't cook and serve up plates at the window without using both arms. I don't know what we'll do if my arm is broken. Feeling is coming back into my fingers. That's good, isn't it?"

"Hmm…probably. I'm sorry, but you'll have to direct me to the doctor's clinic."

She told him where to turn then eyed him warily. "You've become real handy for my daughter."

In his peripheral vision Seth saw her frown. "Lila juggles a lot of chores, as do you," he said. "Is my chipping in a problem?"

"Depends."

"On?" Seth asked. "Do you have something against me?"

"It's nothing personal, but I've seen a lot of men come and go around here. Life's already handed Lila enough lemons. I'm just saying…"

The local clinic came into view and Seth spotted the Emergency entrance. He certainly got Doreen's message, but didn't know how to respond. "I'll pull up to the door, come around and help you out. I'll park while you check in. I can help if you need me to fill out any forms."

"Why are you being so nice? I just accused you of being a lemon in my daughter's life."

"Zeke, Myra and Lila all tell me this is a neighbor-helping-neighbor town. My time is my own at the moment," Seth said, guiding the woman out. Holding her purse, he walked her through the sliding doors. "This way you didn't have to wait on a cab. And it frees Lila up to open the café on time." Smiling, he draped her purse strap over her good arm.

Afraid it was going to be a long, tedious morning in Doreen's company, Seth nevertheless hurried to park. His phone rang before he could enter the building.

"How is she?" Lila asked.

"I let her out at Emergency, parked and now I'm headed in to fill out papers. She injured her right arm. I'll call you or have her do it after she sees a doctor. Try not to worry."

"Her right arm. Oh, geez. You probably think we should've covered this base in advance since she and I rely so heavily on each other. It's never been necessary. We've both been in excellent health, don't take vacations and work holidays. Unfortunately we both run our operations on a shoestring."

From the wobble in her voice Seth imagined she barely held back tears. "You have friends I'm sure you can call on. But let's get a report first, okay?"

"I do have friends. Jewell leaves for DC soon and has her work piled up until she leaves. Myra's car is in the shop. Tawana's in the Wolf Point hospital scheduled for emergency gall bladder surgery. In fact, I'm supposed to check on her and take her flowers today from the Artsy Ladies because Shelley and Mindy can't." Her voice held a modicum of hysteria. "Now, I don't know how I can do that. Perhaps I can have them delivered. But that's so impersonal."

Seth paused at the ER door. "Tawana's having surgery? Hunter had big plans to show her and Jewell around DC. Do you think someone will call him? Or will she still be able to go with Jewell?"

"I don't know. Shall I add that to my growing out-of-control to-do list?"

"I'll call him later. The guys all gave me their numbers in case work took me in their directions. Listen, I see your mom talking to a receptionist who just handed her a clipboard. Need to go. I've got this end, Lila. I can probably take Tawana flowers. Stay cool, okay?"

"I think you're an angel in disguise," she said, followed by a quick "G'bye."

Smiling, Seth pocketed his phone and went inside.

Doreen met him. "I've never been helpless like this. Why are you grinning? Do you think this is funny?"

"No, ma'am. Lila just phoned. I'm smiling because I think...hope I calmed her concerns. Shall we sit? I'll write if you tell me what to say."

"I hate a stranger knowing my private business," she grumbled.

"In ten minutes I'll have forgotten it all." He let her choose a chair then sat beside her. Only one other man sat in the waiting room. "Okay, they start by asking insurance info. Do you have a card or know the numbers off the top of your head?"

She dug in her purse and removed a wallet. "You'll have to find my card. It may be behind my business license."

Seth retrieved the card and swiftly worked through the general health questions.

"You have nice handwriting for a man," Doreen said. "My husband's writing looked like turkey tracks. But he started to work in the mines at sixteen and never finished high school."

Secretly Seth thought that was sad. But in countries where he hunted gems, kids even younger than that frequently did difficult jobs. He completed the four forms. "Do you feel like returning this to the clerk or shall I?"

"Do you mind? Strangely how I'm sitting causes less pain to my neck and shoulder."

"Then stay. They may want to run a copy of your insurance card. I'll bring it right back." He stood and went to the counter.

The receptionist scanned each sheet. "Everything's in order. I don't need the card." She handed it back. "A nurse will take your mother to X-ray now."

"I'm a family friend," Seth said. "I'll wait over there." He pointed. He'd barely sat and returned the card to her wallet when a nurse came over with a wheelchair.

"I can walk," Doreen declared.

"House rules," the nurse said and glanced at Seth. "The clerk tells me you aren't a relative, so please wait here."

"Good." Seth sank back in his chair. He took out his phone and texted Zeke, bringing him up-to-date. His twin texted right back saying Myra would have her car the next afternoon and could help Lila at home or at the café.

Seth phoned Hunter Wright to let him know about Tawana.

"Thanks, but I spoke to her last night. We're both sorry she won't be able to come to DC, but she's ignored prior attacks. Now tests indicate her gall bladder may be gangrenous. So if one of the ladies in their group visits her I'd appreciate knowing that she's following doctor's orders. I sense she's super independent."

"That description fits several of the women in their group. I may take her flowers from them today." He went on to explain about Lila's mother and the other women's problems tying them down. "How are you? Have they given you a new prosthetic?"

"I just had another surgery. Hopefully I'll get the new leg soon. When are you leaving Snowy Owl Crossing?"

"I don't know," Seth murmured, picturing Lila as they'd played ball with Rory. "I'm following up on the sapphires Gavin mentioned. Tomorrow I may take a look at one of the mines. I applied for a permit to hunt gems, but it'll take time for the state to consider my request."

"So, hey. If you strike it rich you may still be around when I whip this leg into shape and come back there."

"Maybe. Odd how many of Zeke's groomsmen like it here. Hey, Hunter, I'm in a hospital waiting room and the receptionist is giving me the stink eye." The men signed off. Expecting a long wait, Seth sorted through the magazines. Most were old. They ranged from farm news to hunting and fishing, to a couple of dated women's magazines. He closed his eyes thinking he'd grab a nap. And he did nod off until voices jarred him awake.

A doctor in a white lab coat was speaking with Doreen, whose right arm was in a sling.

Seth didn't see a cast and she wore a smile. Rising, he checked to make sure his shirt was tucked in before he walked toward them.

The doctor tore a prescription off a pad and handed it to Doreen. She resisted taking it, but the doc tucked it in her purse.

"I recommend filling it to have on hand."

"I thought I could use ice. You said I have a high tolerance for pain."

"You do, but you gave the elbow quite a whack. It'll hurt to flex."

She thanked him and turned to Seth.

"So, you got good news?" He took out his key and stepped aside to let her exit first.

"Nothing's broken. I hit squarely on my crazy bone. The fatty tissue swelled. That's why I couldn't feel my fingers. My shoulder and upper arm are bruised. It caused the pain to radiate into my neck. But, basically, I lucked out."

"Great. Once we get in the car I'll ring Lila on my cell so you can ease her mind."

"I'm not sure how eased she'll be. The doctor said I can't stir or lift anything over two pounds for a week. I'll be able to carry plates, one at a time, to customers, but Lila will need to cook."

Seth unlocked the car and helped her in, wondering how Lila could add that to running the B and B. Shouldn't her mother see that?

Going around the hood to get in, he clipped her seat belt and followed through on his promise to dial Lila.

"This won't take long," Doreen said, taking the phone. "She'll be busy with the breakfast crowd. I'll let her know we'll be there in a few minutes. When the crowd thins, I can fill her in."

True to her word, she announced they were on their way then said goodbye.

"Do we need to find a pharmacy to fill your script?"

"It's a painkiller. I'm not filling it. Every one I've ever had messed with my head. All I need is to miss a step and fall down my stairs."

"It's your call. I prefer to go with something over-the-counter myself."

"Do you get hurt a lot hunting gems?"

"Some. Rocks slide." Seth was reluctant to bring up the dangers of climbing in or out of old mine shafts, since both Doreen's and Lila's husbands had died in them.

Seth drove slowly toward the café. He thought he might have to double park to drop her close to the café, but it was his lucky day. A car very near the front door pulled out, leaving him the perfect spot.

"You don't need to go in with me," she said when Seth turned off the motor. "Thanks for driving me to the hospital, but I'm sure you have other things to do."

Her tone sounded dismissive to Seth, making his response a tad sharp. "Yes, I do have things to do. One is to run an errand for Lila. Jewell asked her to take flowers to Tawana. But maybe you weren't aware that she had gall bladder surgery today."

Doreen frowned. "Why is Lila in charge of flowers? And why would she ask you to buy them and not one of the other women in her craft group?"

He ticked through the reasons keeping the other Artsy Ladies from going. "So I'll walk in with you and see what kind of a bouquet she has in mind. And ask if she needs anything else done at the B and B while she's busy filling your shoes." But as he circled the car and opened the passenger door, he saw how hard it was for Lila's mother to protect her arm and climb from the vehicle. He underwent a pang of regret over his tone. She didn't know him, after all.

Suddenly solicitous of her condition and what had to be concern for her only child, Seth settled Doreen's handbag on her uninjured shoulder and rushed to open the café door.

At once customers left their tables and gathered around her, commiserating over her injury and asking about her prognosis.

Seth slipped past them and went into the kitchen, where Lila hovered over a hot grill sizzling with bacon, pancakes and fried potatoes. She wore a too-big apron tied with a sagging bow in the back, and her pretty dark hair was covered by a tan net affair. Even viewing her slender frame from behind spread warmth through Seth's body. Tendrils of her hair, which had escaped their confines, moved him to loosely span her waist with his hands and brush a kiss on the exposed flesh below her ear.

She yelped, spun around and almost decapitated him with a large, greasy spatula. "Seth! You scared me half to death. Did you kiss me? Why? And where's Mom?"

Smiling indulgently, Seth released her. "I kissed you because you look so kissable in that getup. But you'd better see to someone's food before it burns. Your mom got waylaid by customers. I expect she'll be here soon."

Lila turned immediately to dish up the breakfast items. "Do you know Joe Watson? About your age but beefier. Black hair. I think he's wearing a red-plaid shirt. Could you deliver this and freshen his coffee? His brother just came in, stuck his head in the window and ordered the same thing but with double bacon."

Because she was obviously frazzled, and he still

tingled from the kiss, Seth took the plate, grabbed the coffeepot off the warmer and found the man he had met once at his brother's wedding. "Joe, Lila sends this and hot coffee. She's starting on your brother's meal." Seth set the plate down in front of the surprised man and deftly topped up his coffee.

"You're Zeke Maxwell's twin," Mark Watson exclaimed and held up his cup for more java. "Waiting tables is a far cry from roofing Zeke's barn."

"Yeah. Guess I'm a jack-of-all-trades. Truthfully—Zeke's helping someone brand calves. I'm staying at Lila's B and B and offered to help when her mom slipped and fell this morning. You're lucky she didn't ask me to open the café. I'm the world's worst cook."

Lila stuck her head out the opening and called to Seth, "Can you give Mark his plate since you're out there?"

"I wonder what she did before I showed up," he joked at large.

"She called customers to the window to pick up their plates. I can get mine," the younger Watson said and did just that.

Seth filled coffee cups on his meandering return to the kitchen.

Doreen had managed to break away from her sympathizers. She entered the kitchen ahead of Seth and, because it appeared Lila had a lull in orders, launched into relaying what the doctor had found. She wound down saying, "I can only wait tables for a week, but I'll only be able to carry one plate at a time. You'll have to cook and handle cleanup, honey. We're lucky I didn't break anything."

Lila looked aghast. "Mom, I have four fishermen booked next week for the steelhead contest. They've rented from me the past two years and expect breakfast and boxed lunches, and like their rooms cleaned daily. Plus, Rory has his heart set on playing on a Little League team and practice starts soon."

Seth watched Lila rub her temples, and he wanted to ease her tension. But both women seemed to have forgotten he was there until he spoke. "Is your high school student available? Can she help wait and bus tables? Cooking, though? I don't have any suggestion for that."

"This is something for Lila and me to work out. Weren't you taking Tawana flowers?" Doreen said pointedly.

"Geez. I totally forgot about that." Lila retrieved her purse from a cabinet. "I need to give you money, Seth, for flowers and for the ball equipment you bought Rory. Oh, I hate to ask, but can you go by the Owl's Nest and unlock Ghost's doggy door so he has the run of our enclosed yard? I lock the door at night to keep him in and away from the risk of wild animals. I flew out so fast this morning, I forgot. My bad."

"Give me a limit on flowers. I'll use my credit card. We can settle up later."

Lila blinked. "Thanks. Oh, one other thing. Rory's afraid with what all I asked you to do that you might not be here this afternoon to play catch with him in the park. And, truly, I've imposed on you too much."

"I said I would play catch with him this afternoon. Of course it'd be more fun if you joined us like you did yesterday."

Doreen flashed a glance between the two. "Lila, you played catch with them? Whatever for? You're a businesswoman. What might your other guests think if they see you out chasing after baseballs?"

"That I'm a mother first," Lila said. "The Owl's Nest is our home. Why wouldn't I make time to play with my son?"

Her mother delivered Seth a dark look. "It's unseemly to cavort around your yard with a renter. If word gets around that you're too chummy with one, it'll give folks a bad impression." She continued to pin Seth with her gaze. "You've never said exactly how long you plan to be in Snowy Owl Crossing until you go back to rock hunting. I'm sure you'll want to have a care to not ruin Lila's reputation."

Lila gasped. "Mo…th…er!"

Seth held up a hand. "I'll leave you ladies to discuss how to handle your workload. After I see to Ghost, I think I'll ask Myra to help me choose flowers for Tawana. Lila, tell Rory I'll be back to go to the park no later than three."

He still wasn't sure what he'd done to irritate Lila's mother, who clearly wanted to drive a wedge between them. Too bad. The more time he spent around Lila, the more he wanted to see what might develop, and he was equally determined to not let her mother spoil that.

Lila's face softened. "Seth, I hope you know the rose you gave me says you don't need help picking flowers for a lady."

Lila's comment would surely set her mom off again, but it made Seth smile as he left.

Chapter Six

Lila waited until Seth was out of earshot before she pounced on her mother. But Doreen beat her to it. "He gave you roses? If that isn't suspect enough the man's leading you down the garden path, I don't know what is."

"He bought a rosebush to set by my front door. The peach blooms say welcome to all of my guests. It was a thoughtful gift."

Doreen harrumphed. "It's a snow job, and you're too smitten to see."

"Mother, this negativity toward Seth is not like you. You've made the café a success because you greet everyone who walks in the same way. You make folks, whether locals or strangers, feel at home. Seth helped us out of a bind today by driving you to the doctor. You got treatment much faster than if you'd had to wait for me. Plus, his volunteering to take you allowed me to open the café on time."

"I'm sorry." Doreen looked contrite for the first time. "It's you I'm worried about, honey child. You and Rory."

"You wouldn't worry so much had you seen Rory's joy last night after Seth gave him only a few pointers on how to throw and catch. He actually improved and his eyes sparkled with a light I haven't seen in… well, too long."

"Yours, too," Doreen said, sounding sour again.

"My eyes?" Lila rubbed at lids she thought must reflect permanent distress. Because for a long time now she'd felt she'd barely kept one step ahead of having everything fall apart in her life, and therefore her son's, too.

"Lila, it's impossible not to see the way you perk up any time that man's around. He is nice and polite. And he's helpful. But at his core even his brother says he's a ramblin' man. Maybe the word Zeke used was 'nomad,' but it means the same."

"Ah, I see. On the basis of one comment you're lumping him in with Clay Shafer. Mother, you have no idea if Seth has staying power."

"Neither do you." Doreen compressed her lips. "I'm only trying to save you heartache, but you're not listening. Oh, do what you will. Just don't come crying to me to help pick up the pieces."

"You're assuming I'll have reason to fall to pieces. I'm a grown woman."

"And you're acting as if being grown up is some kind of insurance against heartbreak. I assure you it's not. But that's the last thing I'll say on this subject. No man is worth splitting up a family over, Lila. We've weathered too much together."

"Agreed. Look, seems like we have a lull in traffic. Want to discuss ways to run the café and my bed-and-breakfast until you've healed?"

"Hank Watson's wife, Sarah Jane, is the only person I can think of who can cook for a crowd. She has no need to work, but at the last potluck she actually said to call her if I ever wanted a break from the café."

"Awesome. Why don't you go upstairs, give her a call and then take a little rest? I'll clean up from breakfast and get lunch under way."

"I am weary. What if I ask Sarah Jane to cover breakfast and overlap a bit when you come in to handle lunch? Also, after high school lets out for summer next week, Becky would like more hours."

"She's a hard worker. Okay, I'll keep my fingers crossed it all works in our favor for a change."

SETH DROVE BACK to the Owl's Nest, unlocked Ghost's doggy door and filled his inside and outdoor water bowls. Delighted to be free, the dog chased a squirrel that had come into the fenced yard. Seth made sure the back gate was locked. On his return trip he locked up the house before phoning his sister-in-law. "Myra, hi. It's Seth. Are you swamped with work or can I ask a favor?"

"Unless it requires a car. Mine's in the shop. Otherwise I'm only painting one of my dollhouses for our next bazaar."

"Here's the deal. Jewell asked Lila to take flowers to Tawana. But then Lila's mom slipped and wrenched her shoulder. Lila asked me to take over flower detail.

Since the flowers will be from your group, I thought it'd be nice if you helped choose a bouquet."

"Hold up. There, I put down my paintbrush. I must've missed something. Aren't the flowers for Doreen? Tawana and Jewell should be preparing to go to DC."

"Jewell has to go alone." He reported on Tawana's unexpected surgery. "I could buy Lila's mom flowers, too. Except she'd think I'm trying to bribe her into liking me."

"Okay, this is a lot to unpack. Why would Jewell ask Lila about flowers? We all know Lila is the busiest one of us."

"I don't know. Wait… I do. I recall Lila knew you had no car. And the other two ladies in your club have other obligations. So, can I pick you up?"

"Sure. Give me a bit to put my paint away."

They agreed on a time. And because he had a few minutes, Seth wrote a note to leave on the door for Lila's other guests, telling them about Doreen's accident. He knew the two couples were checking out. He said they'd find Lila at the café.

Half an hour later when he swung by the ranch for Myra, she climbed into the car bubbling over with new details on Tawana. "She's out of recovery, but her surgery wasn't the simple Band-Aid kind. Silly woman ignored her symptoms so long she got gangrene."

"That's bad."

"Yes, they had to flush her abdominal cavity and put in drains. She'll be hospitalized up to a week.

I'm glad you called and asked me to go see her. Zeke heard the news at the ranch where he's helping out. He figured I could use his vehicle and run over there tonight. Of course, he didn't know about the flowers."

Seth listened as he drove to the nursery where he'd bought Lila's rosebush.

The minute he and Myra walked into the store, the clerk recognized him. "Are you back for another rosebush?" she asked and included Myra in her smile.

"Cut flowers I think," Seth said, deferring to Myra.

The woman pointed to a large, glass-fronted cooler stocked with all types and sizes of bouquets.

"You bought Doreen a rosebush?" Myra asked Seth. "Sorry, I thought you didn't buy her anything?"

Fidgeting, Seth ran a finger inside the neck of his T-shirt. "I, uh, gave Lila a rosebush to set by the front door at the Owl's Nest."

Myra's eyes widened. "Hmm. You sly dog. I feel so out of the loop. Tawana said Hunter sent her pink carnations. What all went on at my wedding that I missed?"

"We're here for flowers," he reminded.

"At least Tawana admitted she likes Hunter and had planned to visit him in DC. You're just being coy."

Seth walked to the flower case and studied the contents. "How about the vase with the multicolored flowers?"

"That vase is cut crystal. It's more expensive than the bouquet in it," the clerk called out.

"It's pretty," Myra said, "but fancier than Tawana's

apartment. Her furniture is leather and her décor is Native American. That turquoise vase with the white and yellow irises will go nicely in her place or in her office at the reservation headquarters."

"See, that's why I needed your help," Seth said and gestured to the clerk with a credit card he'd removed from his wallet.

"Why are you paying?" Myra asked. "Oh, right, Jewell is keeper of the group's funds. Make sure you give her that receipt."

Seth stepped aside to let the clerk retrieve the bouquet. Going to the counter, he set his card atop it. "Okay. I was going to give it to Lila. Yesterday I picked up some baseball equipment for Rory on her behalf and she asked me to add the cost of flowers to the bill. We'll settle up later."

"Then Rory gets to join Little League?" Myra gazed expectantly at Seth as the clerk rang up the flowers.

"I assume so." Seth put back his card, smiled at the clerk and picked up the vase. "I know Lila was worried about cost, but I hope I showed her she didn't need to buy expensive equipment."

"I thought she had a problem getting him to Wolf Point for some practices and League games."

Seth opened Myra's door and, after she'd buckled in, passed her the flowers.

"I don't know anything about that. Can't he ride with his friend?"

Myra shrugged. "Maybe. Let's go back to the issue of the rosebush you so neatly sidestepped. Tawana said Hunter wants to settle here. What's your plan? Lila is one of my best friends."

Seth scowled. "What the hell? Do I look like a big bad wolf? Why do I get the feeling you're ready to put up roadblocks like Lila's mother? Wait, has Zeke indicated I'm untrustworthy or something?"

"No, nothing like that. Zeke loves you and would be delighted to have you settle here. He also told me gem hunting can be dangerous. So far as I know, he wouldn't have shared that with anyone like Lila's mom. I do have concerns for Lila, because she lost her dad and husband to mining. Do you mine for gems? You could get injured doing that."

He parked at the hospital before turning to stare at Myra. "Asks a person who fell over a steep cliff. If I got this right, you fell trying to climb on your horse while holding a calf."

She winced a tad. "And what's your point?"

"Oh, I don't know. That no aspect of life is totally risk free? Lila skidded on a slick highway and put her car in a ditch. Her mother slipped on a puddle in her walk-in cooler. She's lucky she didn't break something vital."

"Those are accidents. You climb mountains rife with rock slides or rope into abandoned mines. You go looking for danger, if you ask me."

"I go looking for gems to earn a living. Is ranching totally safe, Myra?" Seth turned off the motor and jerked out his keys. "Why don't you take your friend her flowers before they wilt? I'm going to see if they have a cafeteria where I can grab coffee and a sandwich."

"You don't want to go visit Tawana?"

"I barely know her. I'm sure she can do without a stranger barging in when she's not feeling a hundred percent."

Myra unclipped her seat belt and shoved open the door. "You're PO'd at me, I can tell. And Zeke will tell me to butt out of your business, too. Lila may say the same. Erase this conversation. She's capable of deciding who to let close."

"I'm not mad at you. It's that your warnings and Doreen's are premature. But they make me want to prove you both wrong. Do I admire Lila? *Yes*. Do I think I can lighten her load a bit and teach Rory a few things about baseball? *Yes*. Am I invested enough to chuck my job? *Maybe. Or maybe not*. By the way, I filed for a state permit to hunt for sapphires around here and gave your address. They may or may not issue a permit, but if I get mail, hang on to it, please."

"Of course we will."

They'd reached the main entrance to the hospital, and Seth stepped around Myra to open the door and let her pass.

"I'm glad we cleared the air," Myra said. "I'd hate to begin married life on bad terms with Zeke's family. Eat slowly," she added, tossing him a smile. "I may come join you for lunch."

Seth nodded and then followed the signs pointing downstairs to the cafeteria.

He ate a sandwich and drank his coffee, but Myra

didn't show up. After an hour Seth elected to go in search of her.

He got directions to Tawana's room on the surgical wing, and he could hear the sounds of friends yakking away about their holiday bazaar projects even before he entered the room. Zeke had told Seth about the bazaar where the women sold crafts as a fund-raiser to band and keep track of the snowy owls.

He didn't step fully into the room, but rather leaned in far enough to catch Myra's attention. Seth tapped his watch. "Hey, you're long past lunch. I need to get you back to the ranch. I promised Rory another baseball lesson at three o'clock."

Myra stopped midsentence to gape at him. "Mercy, is it that late?" She stood. "Tawana, you remember Zeke's twin brother?"

The woman in the bed offered a smile. "Hunter tells me you may stay in Snowy Owl Crossing."

Seth shrugged. "The guys in the wedding party all like it here. Only Hunter committed to coming back once he gets past a couple of surgeries of his own."

"Yes, but I was just telling Myra, he's signed up to take a leather-working class at the VA. I do vests and belts. He's starting with wallets, but said his instructor tools pictures on leather, paints and frames them. Hunter's excited to learn that. Says maybe it's something he can do to supplement his military disability pay after he moves here."

Seth entered the room and tucked a thumb under his belt. "I can vouch for your belts. Zeke sent me one for Christmas. My friends in Australia all asked where I got it. I don't know if there's a market for leather artwork, but you could set up an online store and make some money selling these belts."

"Hey, great idea. Maybe we could all do that," Myra said. "I bet we could earn more money to save the snowy owls."

"You ladies are sure dedicated to those birds. One dive-bombed us when we pulled Lila's Jeep out of the ditch. Another swiped Rory's brand-new baseball. Plucked a ball I'd thrown Lila right out of the air. I wouldn't think you'd be so enamored of them, Myra. You and Zeke told all of us how an owl almost made off with your pet pig."

"One really snatched a baseball?" Tawana asked.

"You made that up," Myra accused.

"I swear it happened. If you don't believe me, ask Lila. The only other birds I've seen steal stuff were two big crows in Italy that claimed my slice of sausage pizza."

"Owls are born hunters. I'm sure the bird thought the baseball was prey."

"Our snowy owls are revered by my people," Tawana said earnestly. "But Jewell knows their numbers have dwindled. They need a safe habitat."

Myra went to stand at the door with Seth. "Don't fret, Tawana. We'll get a sanctuary even if we have to buy land. And, Seth, I may owe the very fact that Zeke saved my life to a snowy he says convinced him to take the right fork in the trail."

Seth threw up his hands. "I get it. Listen, we need to go. Considering what you've been through, you look good, Tawana. But we shouldn't tire you. In the morning I'm taking one of Lila's horses to scope out a mine for sapphires. But if you're here the day after and Myra still has no car, I'll be happy to bring her for another visit."

"What mine?" the women said in unison.

Seth shrugged. "Opportunity. It's been closed a long time. The state owns it now. The last gem hunters spread rumors that it's haunted." He glanced up and noticed both women frowning. "Don't tell me you believe in ghosts?"

Tawana turned her head and punched a button to lower the head of her bed.

Myra continued to have a furrowed brow as she said, "Goodbye," then none-too-gently hustled Seth from the room. In the hallway she said, "You should stay clear of that mine." Head up, she marched to the elevator. "It claimed the lives of an entire mining crew. One being Lila's husband." She stabbed the elevator button repeatedly.

Seth followed her into the empty car. "I'm sorry for the tragedy, but gemstones are often found in defunct shafts," he said, quickening his steps to keep up as Myra left the elevator. "Poison gas can be an issue, but if the state gives me a permit, I have equipment to explore safely. I'm careful. I don't disturb old scaffolding. I'll look for specific rock formations. Crystals and such, not gold or copper. Sapphires sell for a tidy sum. What's bad about that?"

"Nothing to me. But do you honestly think Lila would look on you favorably?"

Seth struggled, trying to picture Lila's reaction. He liked her. He wanted her to like him back. But he was who he was. "Until I have a permit in hand and am at a point to say 'Yes, I'm going to look for sapphires in Opportunity Mine' or 'No, I'm not,' is there any reason to worry Lila?"

They reached the car. "I have another question, Myra. If one person cares for another, shouldn't they accept them as they are? I've been a gem hunter for a dozen years."

Myra appeared to give that some hard thought as she buckled up. "That's a tough one, Seth. I'm no expert on love, but I believe love is give and take. Did you know your brother was ready to walk away and leave the ranch my folks had given him because my brother told him I expected to inherit it? He loved me that much."

"Okay, this has gotten too deep for me. Who said anything about love?" Seth started the car. "Lila and I are barely past the getting-acquainted stage." He recognized his laugh sounded nervous. Luckily, though, Myra laughed, too.

"So it isn't love at first sight for you two, like with Hunter and Tawana?"

"We just like each other," he rushed to say. But recalling the kiss he'd planted on Lila's neck in the restaurant, and admitting his heart gave a funny, happy kick whenever their paths crossed, he worried that he might be lying to his sister-in-law.

A series of loaded grain trucks slowed their progress. Seth turned down the ranch lane to the Flying Owl and saw that he'd be later than three to meet Rory.

"Thanks for taking me to the hospital." Half in, half out of the car, Myra paused. "All this time we've been talking and I forgot Zeke asked me to tell you he wants to start roofing the barn day after tomorrow. Can you be here by seven? He said we'd check on cattle first. I told him I'd do that alone, but he likes us to share chores." She blushed a bit and, if Seth wasn't running late, he'd tease her.

"I've just been waiting to get word on starting the roof. Tell him I'm not available for long days. Because, like today, I'm sort of teaching Rory to play ball after school."

"Zeke can't very well complain since he suggested you help Rory."

"That's right. But it's helping the kid, so I'm glad Zeke mentioned it."

They said their goodbyes and Seth headed for the highway again.

It was a quarter past three when he found street parking and jogged to the café. The first thing he saw was Rory standing inside the entrance looking anxious, his new mitt and ball in a vise grip against his skinny chest.

The instant the boy saw Seth, his eyes lit up and his shoulders squared. "Mom, Mom," he shouted as he rushed toward the pass-through where Lila had set out two steaming plates. "Seth's here! We're gonna go to the park. We're goin' to the park, Mom!"

Seth banked a smile over the fact Rory had to make every statement twice. He stepped up to the kitchen door and again experienced a funny little punch to his chest from merely seeing Lila, even though she looked hot and rumpled. "Sorry I'm late," he said. "There was some truck traffic and I had to take Myra home. We delivered the flowers to Tawana together. She liked them and is doing well. How's your mother?"

"Okay, I think. She's upstairs now. It's hard for her to watch other people do her job." She blotted sweat from her forehead with the tail of her apron. "I'm glad to see you, because Mom delighted in thinking you weren't going to show up. I can't believe she'd want Rory disappointed. I'm sorry she's not nicer to you, Seth."

He tugged on his lower lip with thumb and finger, but said nothing. It didn't surprise him to hear that Doreen expected him to flake out, but he was happy Lila thought better of him. He hadn't expected that. "We'll go across to the park and play catch until you close, or dark, whichever comes first."

"Or unless Rory makes a nuisance of himself first," Lila said, turning away to flip three hamburgers cooking on the grill.

"I'm not gonna be a nuisance," Rory declared. He'd come in to tug on Seth's shirttail and stayed long enough to barge past him and respond to his mother.

"Come on, slugger. It's never good to contradict your mom."

"What's 'contradict' mean?" the boy asked as Seth hustled them both out of the café.

The few words that came to mind might also be unfamiliar to a nine-year-old. Seth settled on saying, "Sometimes it's simply a safer bet to keep quiet." He stopped at his rental vehicle and got his mitt out.

"All right. But I don't wanna be a nuisance. I know what that is. It means, like, bug you. I want you to teach me more about baseball 'cause Kemper told his coach I'm getting better. Coach said maybe you'll bring me to the school ball field tomorrow afternoon. Memaw said I shouldn't ask. She even told my mom not to ask you." Rory jogged along to keep up with Seth's longer stride as they crossed the street at the light. "Am I bugging you?" the kid asked, a tremor of uncertainty lacing his voice.

"No, Rory. I don't want you or your mom to feel bad about asking me. If it's something I'm not able to do, I'll say so. I have plans for part of tomorrow, but I can easily arrange my horseback ride for the morning. That'll leave my afternoon free. But did you clear my going along to your school practice with your mother?"

"Not 'xactly. I think her and Memaw bickered some more."

"Well, we'll check later. This looks like a clear spot to play catch." They split up and Rory threw the first ball. The play soon grew repetitious for Seth, while Rory's energy never flagged.

After an hour Seth said, "I'm thirsty. We should've thought to bring water."

"The park has a drinking fountain," Rory said, and pointed toward some tennis courts.

"If it's not far, let's hike over and get a drink."

"Yeah. Does your arm get tired throwing? Mine kinda is." Again Rory skipped to stay abreast of Seth.

"You don't want to overdo it. It's a good idea to mix throwing and catching with batting. Do you know if there are batting cages around here?" Seth stopped by the fountain and let Rory take the first drink.

The boy wiped his mouth and moved aside. "Kemper and his dad practice at the cages. But they're 'spensive." His narrow shoulders slumped. "Mom talked to Mr. Barnes. Then she said it's silly to pay money to bat a ball. But Mr. Barnes is going to buy Kemper his own batting machine."

"The machines are costly, but it's not too bad to rent. I remember spending a lot of time in one. I recall we bought tokens and, depending on how many you bought, the machine gave you *X* number of times at bat."

"Probably. But we don't have much money, Seth."

"I know. Let me check into it."

"'Kay. But I see Mom worrying when she pays our bills."

Seth let the comment slide. It was easy to see how much Rory understood about the family finances. He divided the rest of their time between giving Rory pointers and encouragement, and deciding how he might convince Lila to let him pay for batting practice. He didn't think it could cost more than ten or twelve bucks for a hundred to hundred-fifty pitches from the machine. Well worth having the consistency of the high, low, middle range of pitches for a newbie player like Rory.

By five-thirty Seth saw Rory catching better but rubbing his arm between throws and growing less accurate. "We've probably practiced enough for one afternoon, slugger. Besides, my stomach's growling." Seth hoped by putting the onus on himself for stopping rather than suggesting Rory was weakening would be better for the boy's ego.

"Memaw gave me a snack after school. But I'm kinda hungry, too. I played good tonight, didn't I, Seth?"

"You sure did." Seth set the ball back in Rory's mitt, folded his own over and tucked it under his arm. "A secret to playing well is always keep your eye on the ball and don't let what anybody else is doing distract you."

"You mean like when those two kids with the dog ran past us and I totally missed catching that ball?"

"Exactly like that. At games people wander all over. There's clapping and yelling, and a lot of other things happening. You can learn to tune it all out."

"I hope so. I want to play on a team. Kemper said some kids never play good enough to get off the bench."

"Hmm." Seth thought that sounded a little extreme. Why would parents pay Little League fees if their kids didn't play? Maybe Lila thought that could happen to Rory. Another reason he'd need to get the kid some batting practice.

They crossed the street and entered an empty café.

The entry bell over the door jingled. A young woman was stacking menus and Lila, who stretched up to peer out of the pass-through, visibly relaxed when she saw who'd come in.

The girl stopped and said, "Hey, Rory."

"Hey, Becky," the kid said.

"Your mom's dead on her feet and I served so many trout specials I think I wore a hole in one sneaker. If it's okay with your mom, will you lock the door?"

Lila gave her okay. "And after you lock the door, will you run up and check on Memaw? She hasn't surfaced since she went upstairs. I hope she's okay."

"Can I go later? Me 'n Seth are hungry. Is it too late for mac and cheese? Or Seth said he wanted soup."

"I can fix mac and cheese while you go upstairs," Lila said after rubbing her neck. "Becky, go ahead and clock out. And if you can work from eight to five all next week, I'll name my first daughter after you."

Seth saw the girl's head come up. "Are you pregnant?" she gasped.

Lila laughed. "Mercy, no. There's not even a man in my life. That's an old saying."

"Oh." She sounded mollified. But all the same Seth noticed Becky darting glances between him and Lila. And it surprised him to suddenly suffer a flash of something akin to longing. He actually tried to imagine what a little girl might look like if she shared Lila's rich brown hair and blue eyes, and his blond, green-eyed attributes.

Becky passed Lila her time card and said goodbye, asking Seth if he'd lock the door again after she left.

The request jarred him out of his contemplation enough to hear Rory bounce down the stairs to announce, "I woke Memaw up. She said she'll feel better in the morning."

"That's so not like her," Lila said. "I'll go up and see if she needs to come home with us tonight. Did she seem woozy?"

"I don't think so."

Seth walked into the kitchen. "I'll watch the mac and cheese if you want to go up and check on Doreen."

"I'm sure it's breaking some restaurant rule to let you work in the kitchen."

"I'll wash," he said, grinning at her.

She sighed. "I won't be long. Why don't you two eat first? I'll get to the dishwasher when I'm back down."

"Maybe you need to take a break. When we finish eating, Rory and I can help you wind everything down."

Lila blinked and looked skeptical.

"Mom," Rory said. "You didn't ask if I caught and threw good tonight. And I did." He telegraphed a glance at Seth, requesting his concurrence.

"He did great. You're raising a good little ball player," he said then decided maybe it'd be smart to strike while her defenses were down. "Next on our list is to get him batting practice at a batting cage."

Lila tripped on the first step and hurriedly grabbed the stair rail.

"Whoa, take it easy," Seth cautioned. "Last thing anyone needs is for you to be out of commission. We'll talk in the morning about the cage."

She hurried out of sight without replying.

"Mom had on her serious face," Rory said, downcast. "She'll say no."

"Maybe not. This is almost ready to eat. Will you grab a couple of bowls? And if you know where they keep crackers, that'd be nice, too."

They took their steaming mac and cheese to the dining area, where the lights were turned down. It wasn't long before Seth heard Lila futzing around in the kitchen. He scarfed down his food in a few bites, but told Rory to take his time. "Give me a little while to see if I can talk your mom around," he murmured.

Rory stifled a yawn, but he certainly didn't object.

Seth carried his dishes into the kitchen and rinsed them in the sink.

Lila had her back to him, unloading the dishwasher.

He dried his hands and was unable to resist spanning her narrow waist with his hands again, pressing another kiss on the sweet indentation at the back of her neck.

She tried to turn. This time she wasn't holding a large, wicked-looking spatula, so Seth slowly brought her around to face him without letting go.

"What are you do-doing?" she whispered, attempting to see over his shoulder. "Where's Rory?"

"I'm bargaining for batting practice," Seth replied seconds before he slid his hands up her slender back and anchored her solidly against his chest. Then he doubled down by joining their lips.

He heard Lila's sigh of pleasure before she raised her arms and steadied his head, kissing him back until he broke their lip lock to breathe.

She leaned heavily into him, whispering dreamily, "Anything. Ask me for anything and it's yours."

Seth gazed straight into her softened blue eyes. He ran a forefinger over her mouth, abruptly followed by a pressure brush from his lips. Lifting his head ever so slightly, he said in a labored voice, "So, you're cool with Rory practicing at a batting cage? I don't want to take advantage. Frankly…as much as it pains me to say this…you should probably rescind that blanket offer before I ask for way more than you're prepared to give."

Seeming to come to her senses with a jolt, Lila wiggled out of his arms. "I'm so embarrassed. What must you think?"

He touched her shoulder, enough to gain her full attention. "I think you're lovely. I've wanted to kiss you since the morning you came out to the barn. But I think you're dead on your feet from a long, eventful day. And I'm being a little unfair. That kiss was only partly because I promised Rory I'd talk you into letting him go to a batting cage. The other part was purely personal."

She rubbed her upper arms. "You'd better go. I'll

agree to let him bat at a cage. But my day isn't done, and you've sufficiently scrambled my brain."

Seth wanted to say more. He wanted to smooth things over. But he could see retreat was best. He scooped up his mitt and told Rory to come relock the door after he left.

Chapter Seven

In the morning Seth got up early and set out for the corral to take care of the horses. On the way he met Lila's four new guests. All retired, they were avid fishermen who had a boat attached to their vehicle. One man told Seth this was their third year at the B and B and they intended to catch the biggest steelhead and win the contest. Amid good humor the four climbed into the van.

Seth watched them drive off before continuing on his way. It delighted him when the horses crowded up to the fence to greet him. He took them into the barn to feed and groom. Afterward he turned them out into the grassy corral again and leaned on the fence to watch them cavort like kids at a new playground.

The last person he expected to see after the way they'd parted the previous night was Lila. So he was a bit astounded when she joined him at the fence.

"I missed catching you at breakfast."

Seth let his booted foot slip off the bottom rail. "I came here first. Is something wrong? I locked Ghost's doggy door last night after our run."

"You must have run him hard. He was sawing logs when I got home and looked in on him. But it was funny, his paws were moving as if he were chasing rabbits in his sleep."

"Yeah, well, we ran faster than normal." He stopped short of admitting he'd had some sexual frustration to run off.

"Uh, what you didn't mention last night, something Rory chattered about all the way home…he seems to think you planned to ask me about accompanying him to the regular Little League practice today after school. If you think he's ready, I need to give you a check to pay his fees. But if he's suckered you into any of those things, tell me, please."

Seth forced his thoughts away from how pretty she looked this morning and murmured, "Once I saw you in the kitchen I had other things on my mind."

Lila looked away and cleared her throat. "Should I apologize?"

"Geez, no. Should I? Should I stay away? It's plain your mother thinks so."

"My mother lumps you with a cowboy who became important in our lives when I was about Rory's age. One day he up and left for a job in another state. I hurt for a while. Mom apparently never got over it."

Seth felt the breath leave his lungs. To adjust, he swung away and braced both arms on the fence. "Myra thinks like your mom. Yesterday she said if I'm not staying indefinitely I should keep my distance from you. Or that was the gist. I'll be honest,

Lila. I like it here and I like you. But I can't promise I'll stay. I have to earn a living."

She set her hand on his arm, leaving it until he faced her again. "I told Mom I make my own decisions. I'll tell Myra the same. All I ask, Seth, is that no matter what happens between us, if you leave you'll say goodbye to me and Rory. Clay Shafer took off without a word."

"I'll promise that." Seth took her in his arms then and kissed her with enough desire to erase any doubt lingering in either of them that this was more than a casual friendship.

"Mom!" Rory's shout from the porch abruptly ended their kiss.

"I'm coming, honey," Lila called, tugging down her shirt, which Seth's hands had rucked up.

"Are you asking Seth about ball practice at my school?" Rory yelled.

"Is it okay?" Seth asked, touching her chin. "He needs to play with kids his age. I'm going riding this morning, but I'll be back in time for practice."

"How can I say no? I'm needed even more at the café. But playing ball is all Rory wants to do. With your help he's already gained confidence. I'll tell him okay, and send the school a note giving permission for you to pick him up."

"Good. I never thought of that." Seth set his hand at the back of her waist and walked beside her. It felt so right—so natural he thought maybe Lila was the woman he'd been hoping to find to complete his life. And Rory—the fact she had a really great kid was a bonus.

Since the other guests had gone, Seth joined Rory to eat in the kitchen. He didn't know how a boy who talked nonstop managed to consume eggs and toast. Only after he finished and trucked off to dress for school did Seth get to talk more to Lila. "Because the batting cage was my idea, would you be insulted if I pay for those sessions? Rory said school's out Friday for summer. We could go an hour or so every day before League practice. It would help him tremendously."

"Aren't you working with Zeke to roof their barn?"

"Yes. He wants to start tomorrow. But that shouldn't take more than three days and it won't be all day, either."

"Rory would be in seventh heaven," Lila said slowly. "But you already left too much money at the table for your dinner. I need to give that back."

"Don't. I caused you extra work. Plus, you fit me in. I know ball fees add up. Rory's a good kid. He's concerned about your finances."

Lila bit her lip. "I hate that money's tight, but it is. I can only say thank you. But if it turns out he ties you down too much, please say so, Seth."

"Sure." Her comment caused him to think about the only other call he might have on his time—hunting sapphires if the permit came in. Unexplained guilt shivered up his spine. Should he mention it? But why create potential discord until he knew for sure he'd be going into the old mine? Today he only planned to scout the area.

Lila handed him the check for Rory's fees.

He put it in his billfold. Then, when she said she was running behind and needed to get ready to take Rory to school, Seth studied her. "Do you ever get any time off from the café? I know it's not possible now with your mom's injury. I'm jumping ahead to when Rory may get to play in a real game. Might the person helping Doreen cook in the mornings be able to work an afternoon or two?" He pulled her into a loose embrace.

Lila ran her hands up his chest. "I help Mom every day. When Rory started begging to join Little League I began to see how my juggling two jobs impacts him. In fact it has for a while. Last year Jewell took him to the Wild Horse Stampede in Wolf Point. I wanted to go, but I had guests here and the café was swamped."

She looked so downcast, Seth lifted her chin and kissed her tenderly. "You need to carve out some time for fun," he murmured against her lips.

She sighed. "Fun? I'm not sure I'd recognize it. Wait, I take that back. It was fun the evening we played catch with Rory."

"See?" He hugged her tighter and splurged on another lengthy kiss. "Fun is possible."

"Mmm-hmm," she said, eyes still closed as he straightened away. "It's been a long time since I've done any kissing, too. I was afraid I'd forgotten how."

"Definitely not." Smiling, Seth reluctantly called a halt. Primarily because he felt the effect kissing her was having on a crucial part of his anatomy. It would be so easy to explore with her the kind of fun adults could have in bed. But they weren't at that stage and she had to work. And he had his morning planned. Plus, Rory might bounce in at any minute ready to go to school.

Taking her hands from his chest, Lila made a space and gazed up at him. "Are we embarking on something foolish?" she asked, her voice husky.

He rubbed an eyebrow and waited for her to reach her own conclusion. She had been under his skin from the moment he'd walked her down the aisle at his twin's wedding. Halfway there, as candles flickered and piano music filled the church, he'd fallen under the spell of her sweet perfume and the soft touch of her fingers tucked around his arm. But he hadn't been prepared then for her to feel the same way. Then that first day in the barn he wanted to kiss her and sensed she sort of liked him, too.

As if she'd tapped into his thoughts, she tilted her head and said, "I confess when our paths first crossed I'd hoped to get to know you better. My friends in the wedding party saw and razzed me. So, I guess if it's up to me, I'm game to see what develops."

He expelled a breath. "Me, too. A hundred percent. Except now I'd better hit the trail and quit keeping you from your day." He pressed a last kiss to her forehead and strode to the front door, where he plucked the cowboy hat he'd bought at the airport off the antique hat rack. Putting it on, he realized he'd meant to ask Lila something. With a snap of his fingers he spun back, almost bowling her over.

"Wow, new hat? To swipe Rory's favorite phrase, it looks cool."

"I bought it and the boots when the other guys left. Hey, would it be okay to take Ghost on my trail ride?"

"Sure, if you think he'll behave. There's a rope leash hanging by the saddles."

"I'm not in a rush. And he'll be company for me."

Rory came out then. "Mom, Kemper said we could play catch before school. I need to go now."

Lila said she wasn't quite ready and sent him off to fetch Ghost.

"Are you going to take him for another run?" Rory asked Seth when the excited Lab bounded up.

"I'm riding Merlin into the foothills. I thought Ghost might like the outing."

"But you'll be back in time for my practice?" The boy was clearly anxious.

"Count on it," Seth said then left with the dog.

He caught Merlin and saddled him. It'd been a while since he'd ridden. But the horse had an easy gait. The weather was sunny and breezy. Ghost loped along fine.

As they climbed into the foothills following what remained of a mining road, Seth noticed two large birds circling overhead. He reined in, thinking they were buzzards, thus signifying something dead. On closer inspection with the binoculars he'd slung around his neck, he identified a pair of snowy owls.

"I thought owls were night hunters," he said aloud, drawing a throaty woof from Ghost.

He rechecked his phone's GPS. The owls appeared to be circling directly above the Opportunity Mine. The mine was much closer to town than he'd anticipated.

Moderately concerned the birds' presence meant other people poking around, Seth kept Merlin at a walk. Experience had taught him that if a permit had been issued to another gem hunter, that person wouldn't take kindly to having a stranger barge in.

He approached the mine entrance, but detected no movement. No vehicles were visible. From where he sat atop a shifting horse, he identified a warren of once-active roads now overgrown with brush. The entrance wasn't blocked, which surprised him, though he saw several no-trespassing signs.

Seth didn't spot any perimeter cameras, but that didn't mean none existed. Ultimately he decided against dismounting. He'd wait to explore further once he knew whether or not he'd be granted a permit.

From the articles he'd read at the library, he knew miners had dug into the hill for about five hundred yards before splitting into two shafts. The decision to dig deeper and go beneath the original trenches had been blamed for the collapse. He wondered why the families of those who'd died hadn't sued the owners. Tunneling beneath prior excavations didn't strike him as smart. From the drawings on file, short tunnels fanned out on both levels. Sapphires had been found in one fairly straightforward offshoot.

It wasn't until he decided to ride past the mine to check out a river he could hear meandering through the landscape that he realized the owls had gone. Now everything was still except the river, Merlin and Ghost.

As they traveled along a riverbank strewed with patches of yellow flowers, Seth was struck by the peaceful beauty he recalled his brother so eloquently describing shortly after he'd arrived in Snowy Owl Crossing. Seth thought he could be happy here—providing he could make a living. Helping Lila around the B and B while he was on vacation was one thing. It'd go against his grain to even consider doing that on a more permanent basis unless he contributed to expenses more than paying rent.

Eventually he came upon a low spot where he climbed off Merlin and let both the horse and dog drink from the cold, bubbling water. He sat to enjoy nature and to also think about his future. Depending on whether the mine still held sapphires, how many and what grade, he could conceivably earn enough to last a couple of years. He'd be thirty-four years old. *Then what?* He wasn't without savings. He'd socked a decent amount away with retirement in mind. But not at thirty-four. Along his journeys he'd met a few fairly old gem hunters. Most had bad knees, worse backs and lived from find to find. He'd always known he didn't want to trek the globe forever. He wanted more from life. He wanted a wife and kids. But he'd want to support them or to help support them. And he honestly had no idea what type of job he might do.

He broke off a daisy and stared at its cheery face. Maybe he should have looked into whether or not he'd had what it took to play big league baseball. If he'd made the pros, his career would have ended about now, but he'd be richer. Providing he hadn't gotten injured.

Sobered by his thoughts, he swung back into the saddle and set out at a brisk trot for home. *Only, it wasn't home.*

Once back at the Owl's Nest, he exercised the other horses and mucked out the barn because he liked keeping busy and needed the exercise. But it barely left him time to shower and rush off to meet Rory at his ball practice.

He parked in the school lot five minutes after classes let out. It surprised him to have Rory fly down the steps and nearly knock him off his feet in a massive hug. "Whoa! What gives?" he asked around a laugh as he unwound Rory's arms from his waist and smiled at a teacher.

The teacher said, "He's anxious, Mr. Maxwell."

"I was afraid you'd forget."

"Hey, you need to stop expecting the worst. Is that the field where you'll play?" Seth indicated a field with a mesh backstop.

"Nah. That's for older guys. Come on, I'll show you our ball diamond." He held his mitt in one hand, but latched his other to Seth's larger one.

The duty teacher flashed Seth a smile.

At the field Rory dragged him from parent to parent, telling them all that Seth could've played pro ball if he'd wanted to. It was endearing but also embarrassing.

Seth found it amusing that many of the dads wore suits and ties. And that the oft-touted Kemper Barnes's father had a wimpy handshake.

The coach took Lila's check and glanced down at Rory. "I hope he's improved. Midway through the year I came and observed his age group. I told Matt Barnes to tell Rory's parents not to waste money paying his fees."

Seth, who had a hand on Rory's shoulder, felt the boy slump. Anger that a kids' coach could be so insensitive burned through Seth. "He's improved since he changed his mitt. Up to now we've concentrated on throwing and catching. We'll get to batting soon," he said, smiling down on Rory. "I trust you'll allow for that."

The coach grunted then walked away.

Leading Rory to an empty spot on the bleachers, Seth said, "You'll do fine. Remember to block out the noise, keep your eye on the ball and squeeze your mitt as soon as you feel the ball touch the leather."

"Coach thinks I suck." Rory dug the toe of his shoe into the dirt.

"You don't." Seth pulled a Yankees ball cap out of the side pocket of his cargo pants. "I found this when I bought your mitt. It'll keep the sun out of your eyes until they issue Little League uniforms."

"Oh, boy! Oh, boy! Thanks." Rory dashed off and Seth settled back to watch. The coach hit each player grounders and pop-up fly balls. Seth was proud of

Rory. He missed only one ground ball when it hit a rock and veered off. Batting was a whole other story. Seth groaned the last of the four times the boy struck out.

Then practice was over. Seth was glad to see Rory's enthusiasm hadn't dimmed. And Coach Landis caught them before they left the field. "Maxwell…you've done wonders with the kid's ability to catch. I need an assistant this season. Are you available?"

Still mad at how the jerk had treated Rory, Seth shook his head. "No, thanks. I'm slated to help my brother roof his barn. And I don't really know what the rest of my summer will bring."

"Well, if you change your mind, it's apparent you have teaching talent."

They left. At the front of the school, the other kids called goodbye to Rory.

"Gosh, that's the first time Joel Ross ever noticed me," he said around a big grin.

Seth remembered a time in his youth when some athletes who'd thought they were hot stuff had looked down on newbie players. His dad had made sure he and Zeke never acted that way. Digging out his car keys, he turned toward his vehicle.

"I have my bike," Rory said. "Mom said to ride to the café. If you're going there, maybe we could put the bike in your trunk?"

"Sure thing." Seth glanced at his watch and saw it was almost six o'clock. "I'll grab a burger. Or a salad," he added quickly, noting how Rory beamed.

The kid handed Seth his mitt and ran to unchain his bike.

They'd just got under way when Seth's cell phone rang. He thought it might be Lila, checking on him and Rory. To his surprise the readout said Yoti Shigura, a Japanese friend he sometimes joined on gem hunts. He set the phone on the console and tapped speaker. "Yo," he said, moving into traffic. "What's up?"

"Are you on a dig?"

"Nope. I'm in the States. Came to my twin brother's wedding. I'm about to help roof his barn."

"Get out of it. A dude I know brought a fortune in rubies out of an abandoned iron mine in northern China. They're the color and clarity of old Burmese gems."

"Holy cow! You've seen them cut and polished?" Seth felt the beginning of the usual itch to be in on such a deal. But he happened to glance at Rory and saw the kid slump when Yoti said he had seen them and that Seth should hop a plane to Beijing ASAP.

"Uh, I've committed to another obligation here, Yoti. I'm doing a little baseball coaching." Seth braked his desire to hunt rubies. All he really had to do was to remember how Lila had felt in his arms earlier and then to add how the coach had spoken negatively about Rory in front of him. He wanted Rory to show the guy. "Sorry, but when I give my word on something, I like to keep it."

"Will coaching get you a million bucks?" Yoti persisted, pressuring him.

"Not in cash but in satisfaction," Seth stated firmly. "Listen, thanks for thinking of me. If anything changes, I'll get in touch. Otherwise, I wish you the best of luck."

"Okay, but these are the richest gems I've seen since I started in the business."

Seth suffered a moment's regret but shook it off. "I can say I knew you when you were poor," he joked then said goodbye. He began to look for a parking spot near Lila's Jeep so he could transfer Rory's bike.

"What are rubies?" Rory asked.

"Huh? Oh, they're pricey red stones jewelers set in rings and necklaces."

"That guy said you could make a million dollars. For real?"

Seth shrugged and backed into a spot that opened up beside Lila's SUV. "Yoti's a good judge of gems. But China's a long way from Snowy Owl Crossing. Sometimes a pocket of gemstones is smaller than initial hunters think."

"Do we have rubies in Montana?"

Chuckling, Seth braked and shut off the motor. "Quality rubies are rare to find anywhere, Rory. No rubies here that I know of, but Montana has sapphires. If they're big enough and clear enough, they might net a million. Hey, run inside and get your mom's car key and I'll move your bike over to her SUV."

"Okay. Seth, those gems you say Montana has, are they red?"

"No, they're blue. But you won't find any, Rory. Gemstones don't lie about in the open. They're found high atop mountains or deep in old mines. Hurry now, get that key. I'm starved."

Rory scurried into the café and had returned by the time Seth had the bike out on the sidewalk. "Unlock the hatch," he said. "I'll toss this in."

The boy did as requested. "Mom's cooking. Memaw is going upstairs. She asked me to help Becky clear tables. If you finish eating and leave before I'm done, what time can we go to the batting cages tomorrow? I want to tell Mom."

"I'm helping Zeke start his barn roof in the morning. See if your mom's okay with me picking you up after school. We can hit the cages every day until school's out. Coach said the next League practice is at two o'clock the Monday after school lets out for summer. That should definitely help improve your batting."

Rory fist pumped the air before he opened Seth's car and retrieved his mitt. "Hey, your phone's still on the console," he called over the slam of the hatch.

"Thanks. I should take it so I can touch base with Zeke. Did you happen to notice if there are any booths available?"

"There are. I'll get you one and a menu." He hesitated a minute then gazed at Seth and said, "Nobody but my mom ever gave up stuff to help me before. I love you, Seth." Ducking his head, Rory disappeared into the café.

Time lagged for a moment. The kid had stunned him. In that split second Seth knew he'd been right to refuse Yoti. People in Snowy Owl Crossing had become important to him. Especially certain people.

Deciding to store Rory's sentiment for now, Seth grabbed his phone, locked his vehicle and went inside, making supper the prime issue on his mind.

That lasted until he glanced around and saw Lila framed in the pass-through. Even with her face red from the kitchen heat, and in spite of the silly cap she wore to hide her pretty hair when she cooked, merely glimpsing her caused a tight flutter in Seth's belly. All other sights and sounds in the café faded until Rory, standing by a booth wildly waving a menu, garnered Seth's attention. But the fact Lila saw him, waved happily and smiled, welded him to the spot for another moment while he sorted through and set aside a strong desire to go into the kitchen and kiss her.

Willing his skipping pulse to settle, he finally went to the booth where Rory impatiently waited. "Mom said she has meat loaf. It's good, but it comes with garlic potatoes and yucky green beans," the boy added, making a face.

"Are you taking our orders?"

"Yeah. Becky's washing dishes. Mom said I hafta eat before I help clear tables. I wanted to tell her about practice, but she's busy cooking."

"The café's packed. She'd listen if she could, Rory."

"I s'pose. I wish I could have a cheeseburger." He said it with longing.

Seth studied the menu. "A cheeseburger sounds

good. I'll have that and a dinner salad. Tell your mom I'm not fussy about the dressing."

Rory frowned. "Do you like lettuce, tomatoes and stuff more 'n French fries?"

"Salad is better for my health." *Of course he'd rather have fries. But he wanted to be a good role model.* That, too, struck Seth as something new.

"Okay, I'll have the same." Rory took the menu and scampered off to the kitchen, leaving Seth pleased with himself.

After the order arrived, Rory ate fast. Seth lingered over his meal, hoping to grab a word with Lila. He made his call to Zeke, but when it ended he had no excuse to hang around the café any longer. Again he dropped money on the table and stood.

Lila beckoned him to the pass-through. "Rory's full of talk about today's practice, rubies and China, and you guys going to batting cages." She gestured behind her at steam rising from the grill. "I really don't have time to make sense of it. I hope to be home by eight. Could you join me for tea in the kitchen?"

"Be glad to." Seth's heart sped, knowing he'd still spend a part of the day with Lila. "Meanwhile, I'll see if Ghost wants to run, then I'll feed him."

She smiled but turned back to the grill. On his way out Seth waved to Rory, who was stacking dishes in a gray plastic basin.

Chapter Eight

Seth finished his run, fed Ghost and went up to his room to shower. He and the dog had really bonded. As he changed, he heard the fishermen come in amid a lot of good-natured guy talk. After he dressed, he sat by his window, half reading a magazine on raising horses, half watching for Lila to drive in. He'd been thinking a lot more about other jobs he might be able to do after he'd turned down Yoti's urging without much regret over missing out on rubies.

The minute he saw the Jeep's lights turn off the highway, he dashed downstairs to the kitchen, where he put the teakettle on to heat.

He heard Lila and Rory come inside. They were always caring of guests, so Lila's tone was hushed. Still, Seth understood she and Rory were having a little tiff before the boy caved and trundled off to bed.

Figuring their argument stemmed around batting practice, Seth prepared for Lila's verbal combat as she entered the kitchen. However he reeled from her first words.

"Tell me why you filled my son's head with poppycock about making a million dollars finding rubies or Montana sapphires."

The teakettle whistled, giving Seth a minute to collect his thoughts. He poured boiling water into two mugs that held tea bags, moved them to the table and gestured for Lila to sit. "I didn't fill his head. A friend I sometimes join on gem hunts phoned to update me on a cache of China rubies. Rory and I were on the road so I put the call on speaker phone. Rory heard our conversation."

Lila scowled but finally sat. "Myra told everyone that you broker gemstones and Zeke said you hunted lapis in Afghanistan when he served there. Rory said you find gemstones in mines. He couldn't stop talking about how much money the guy who called said you were giving up. I had no idea."

"Yeah, precious gems start as minerals and they're found in layers of rock or often in old mines. Some, like rubies, diamonds and sapphires, are worth a lot of money."

"I don't give a tinker's damn how much you can earn. With me, mines are totally taboo." She balled her hands on the table and added, "I think it'd be best for everyone if in the morning you find another place to stay."

"Hold on!" Seth reached across the table and took her hand. "I hope Rory told you I'm not meeting my friend because I'm committed to teaching Rory baseball."

Lila tugged loose and gripped her mug. "His second most discussed subject was having you take him to a batting cage. Mostly, though, he raved about blue stones in Montana mines. He said if they were big we could make a million dollars and I wouldn't need to work two jobs."

The breath left Seth's lungs in a whoosh. "Lila, I swear I tried to make clear to Rory what I once told you—gemstones don't lie around waiting to be picked up. I think I only mentioned mines in passing. He assumed a lot. Cross my heart, I refused a chance to earn big money by going to China after reportedly flawless rubies."

"What did you tell Rory about Montana?"

"He asked if there were rubies here. I said no but that Montana has sapphires. I maybe said if they were big and plentiful they could be worth as much as rubies. I thought I stressed that it takes digging to find them. But, yeah, I may've said they show up in old mines, because they do." He frowned over the rim of his mug.

"Do you intend to hunt for them? I couldn't handle that. You may not know my dad died in a mine when I was little. I told you about Kevin. I still jolt awake some nights in a panic, picturing everyone I love trapped deep in a pitch-dark mine. It's terrifying, Seth."

He got up and took her in his arms. Feeling her erratic heartbeat and her jerky breath on his neck, Seth knew she was more important than gems. He lightly brushed his chin back and forth over her silky hair. "Babe, I can't stand to see you so anxious." His hold tightened. "I don't have any clue how else I might earn a living, because I've been a gem hunter since I left university. I have some money saved. At my age it's not enough to last. It's probably enough to allow me to explore other options. Anyway, hunting sapphires here takes a permit, which I don't have," he said firmly.

Lila snuggled closer. "Would you really consider doing something else?"

"I would. For you. I did toy with the notion after Zeke left the military and learned to be a rancher. I don't think cattle ranching is for me, but you make me want to settle here, Lila. I'll see what kinds of jobs companies around here are hiring for."

"I have an idea if you're really open to one… After you left the café, Kemper and his parents came in. Mr. Barnes is impressed by how much you've taught Rory in a short time." Leaning back she gazed up into his face. "I hesitate to mention this. I don't want you to think I'm trying to reorder your life. But… our high school baseball coach plans to retire. Uh, he may also teach science. I know you'd be great in the coaching part."

Seth released her. "Our tea is getting cold. Let's sit again and discuss this further."

She took their mugs and zapped them in the microwave. "It was only a thought."

"I like giving Rory tips," he said after she returned to her chair. "I'd enjoy coaching. As for teaching, I have a masters in geology. And I like science. I wonder what I'd need to qualify to teach in Montana." He spoke almost to himself.

"Myra might know," Lila said. "She used to teach college math. You can ask her tomorrow if you're starting to roof their barn. But, Seth, you have to be sure. If in a couple of years you got restless being in one place and then you left, it'd be harder on all of us than it would be if we agreed to part company now."

"I'm pretty sure that wouldn't happen. People may envy world travelers, but it gets tiresome and old. Unearthing gems kept me going this long but, to be candid, when I talked to Zeke about visiting, part of me yearned to settle down. Once I got here I felt at home. Meeting you and helping Rory is like icing on the cake."

Lila blushed. "No one's ever compared me to frosting before."

Seth studied her intently. "Your lips taste sweeter than frosting. And at the moment I'm imagining tasting you everywhere."

"Please..." She ducked her head. "You...you should know I...don't have a lot of experience. You probably expect more of a woman my age who is a widow. But..."

Seth interrupted by capturing the hand she waved through the air. "Lila, there's no pressure. I see how difficult it is for us to grab a few minutes alone together. I know your home is full of strangers and that you live in close quarters with a son at an impressionable age. Plus, he's observant. It's important that he be willing to share you with me." Seth brought her hand to his lips and pressed a kiss in the palm.

"You're already his hero, Seth."

"Maybe, but boys can be super protective of their moms. I'm okay with slow and steady. Does that suit you?" he asked, curling her fingers to his mouth to kiss.

"Honestly? Sometimes I look at you and feel in a rush for…more."

Seth grinned because no sooner had she spoken than she seemed horrified by what she'd said. "That's good. May I point out that you have a nice hayloft. Or I have a very private end room upstairs."

Lila snatched her hand away and shoved back her chair. "Okay, it's not just hot tea making me sweat. Oh, wait, Seth. We've covered a lot of topics we both need to think long and hard about. And it's late. I need to check on Tawana and see how she's doing."

Quick to take the hint, Seth stood. He bent, dusted a kiss over her lips and felt relieved when she lightly touched his face and didn't pull away. He straightened first, collected his mug and set it in the sink. "It's settled in my mind," he said, going to stand under the archway. "Tomorrow morning I'm helping Zeke. If you're cool with me taking Rory to the batting cages for a couple of hours, I'll pick him up from school. We'll return to the café around five thirty."

"As long as you swear he won't come back filled with pie-in-the-sky schemes to find gems that'll sell for a million dollars."

Seth raised his right hand. "I do solemnly swear."

Lila acquiesced with the barest incline of her chin. It was sufficient, and Seth went upstairs set to start making big changes in his life.

In the morning when he got dressed, his gaze fell on the equipment he'd bought to explore the mine. He might return them, but for now he'd store them in the barn. There was a tool chest in the tack room. The flashlights could be useful in case the power ever went out. He thought he still had the receipt for the lighted helmet and harness with oxygen mask. As soon as he had some spare time he'd see about going back to the sporting-goods store. But before he got too excited about a possible coaching job, he needed to learn what applying entailed.

Toting the gear to the barn, he put everything in the toolbox and closed the lid. Turning, he saw Rory watching him.

"What did you put in the wooden box, Seth? Is it more stuff for Little League?"

"No. What's got you up so early, slugger? Did you come to help me feed the horses?"

The boy shook his head. "Memaw called. She needs Mom to work all day 'cause Mrs. Watson has an appointment she forgot."

Outside a horn honked.

"That's Mom. She put muffins and stuff out for you and the others. We gotta go, but she knows you're picking me up from school." Rory headed for the door.

Seth followed him and waved to Lila as Rory climbed into the Jeep. They drove off and he went back to feed and water the horses. It was too bad there was no market for horses. Raising and training them kind of appealed to Seth. Although, that was what Lila had wanted her husband to do. Seth immediately crossed that off his list. He wasn't a stand-in for Lila's first husband.

After chores he grabbed muffins and coffee to go. Twenty minutes later he drove down the lane to the Flying Owl Ranch. Zeke was already up on the barn roof.

Myra, leaning on a stack of brick-red metal roofing material, hailed him. "Zeke's anxious to get this done before next week's prediction of rain. Ah, good, you came prepared with gloves, sunglasses and ball cap."

"Before I scoot up the ladder, I have a question. Lila tells me the high school coach is retiring. He also teaches science. I…may want to apply. She thought you might know what I'd need to qualify."

His sister-in-law's mouth dropped. "You're not going back to gem hunting?"

Shaking his head, Seth tipped his ball cap over his eyes.

"You'd need a provisional exclusion to teach until you could obtain a certificate in education in addition to your degrees."

"Can I take online classes for that?"

"Yup. Go look at the state education website. It'll list approved online schools. If you set a plan and start classes, a school can issue provisional certification. Schools always need science teachers, especially rural schools. By chance, is this because you're falling for Lila?" Myra slipped in the question and elbowed Seth's arm.

"Would you and the other Artsy Ladies give me the green light?"

"Boy, oh, boy, I would."

"Hey!" Zeke called down. "Did you come to help me or do you plan to jawbone with my wife all day?"

"He's touchy," Seth murmured. "And 'jawbone'? Not a Bostonian term."

"Your brother is wholly Montanan now," Myra said with pride.

"It suits him. And I think it'll suit me," Seth said before mounting the tall ladder braced against the barn.

The brothers worked together stripping off old roofing and tossing it into an open trash bin on the ground. They covered a range of subjects, but Seth didn't share with his twin his growing feelings for Lila Jenkins or his new career plans. They talked baseball. Seth invited Zeke to Rory's games. "Give him a few games to see how well he learns to bat, though. Lila's work schedule will keep her from going to his first few games. It'll do him worlds of good to have someone besides me in the stands rooting for him."

"Text me the dates he plays. I'll try to make a game or two while Myra's building her dollhouses for the Thanksgiving bazaar."

They went on to discuss the bazaar and how the money the women earned went to band and keep track of snowy owls. "Myra wondered if Jewell's still going without Tawana to meet with the House Natural Resource Committee."

"Lila said she is. How angry do you think Leland Conrad will be if the government takes his timberland for owls?"

"Hard to say. I hear he's not well, but I haven't heard what's wrong with him. He did talk to Jewell once about selling the ladies the forest. But his Realtor changed his mind."

"Uh, maybe it'll all work out."

They quit talking and made good progress.

Myra delivered sandwiches and iced tea for lunch, but rode off to check on the cattle.

Climbing back to the roof, the men worked until two o'clock. Then Seth said, "I need to take off to go shower. I'm picking Rory up from school to go to the batting cages."

"Sounds like fun. I wish I had a son," Zeke lamented.

Seth laughed. "I trust you know the stork doesn't bring babies, bro."

"Would it shock you to hear we're trying for a baby this soon after marriage?" Zeke asked after they were on the ground. He kept rubbing the arm Seth knew had been shot up in Afghanistan.

"Wouldn't surprise me at all. Being grandparents could bring the folks back from the Caribbean."

"Yeah. Call me sentimental in my old age, but I'd like nothing better than for my whole family, including you, to live around here."

"I'm thinking seriously about it. Well, see you tomorrow. I've gotta dash."

SETH SQUEAKED IN to collect Rory with two minutes to spare. The boy parted from his friends at the flag pole and ran to where Seth sat parked in the line of parents picking up their students.

Rory tossed his backpack and mitt into the backseat, slammed the door and crawled into the front passenger side. "I brought my mitt, but Mom said I probably wouldn't need it. Do you have my bat?"

"In the trunk. Did you have a good day at school?"

"Nah. School's almost out. Our teacher is trying to stuff our heads full of information we didn't get to in our textbooks."

Seth supposed he shouldn't laugh, but keeping a straight face was difficult.

"Mom said I can't ask you about those blue stones. She got mad at me." Rory jiggled his feet. "She gets all hyper if anybody brings up mines. 'Cause my dad died in one. I sorta remember him. But… I asked my teacher about gems. She told the whole class that rock hounds find agates all over Montana. Some are worth a lot of money, just like your friend said. Rock hounds are people, Seth, not dogs."

"Your focus and mine needs to stick to baseball," Seth said, hoping he sounded stern. "So you play well in your games."

"But to earn big money playing baseball I hafta be way older. Kemper said not many guys from here get picked to play as pros. His dad says that's where players make big bucks."

"That's true, but money isn't everything. You live in a nice house, eat well and your mom bought you that New York Yankees shirt," Seth teased, poking a finger at Rory's favorite tee.

They arrived, went inside the rec center and were directed to the proper area beyond the paintball section. At the gate, Seth looked over the pricing. "What do you recommend for a beginner?" he asked the attendant. The young man made a suggestion.

"You can upgrade any time. I assume it's not going to be a one-time visit."

"I think we'll be here every afternoon for a while."

Rory's head bobbed back and forth between the two men until Seth ran his credit card and was given a key to a specific cage.

A few other machines were in operation and Rory fell behind as he peered through the fencing. "The machine pitches," he whispered to Seth.

"Yes. And it can be set to change up balls and strikes, which helps you learn what balls to swing at."

"I wish I had one of these at home," Rory said, following Seth into their cage.

"They cost several thousand dollars, which is why few kids own one and so many come here."

"If I found sapphires and sold them for a million bucks, I could buy my own."

Seth chose to ignore Rory's statement. Instead he went about explaining how the pitching machine worked. "I'll set it for all strikes to start, so I can watch your swing and help you adjust. Our second hour we'll do changeups. Keep your eye on the ball, just like catching. Don't be distracted by folks talking in the next cage or the noise of their machines."

At first Rory was awkward. He pouted when he missed. Seth guided him gently and was pleased when he quickly got the hang of batting. "You're doing great," he said at the end of the session.

"This is fun. Can't we stay longer?"

"I told your mom when we'd be back to the café. We'll come back tomorrow."

"Okay," Rory drawled, skipping along in Seth's wake. "I like this bat a lot. I never hit anything with Kemper's 'spensive green bats."

Seth tugged on the bill of Rory's ball cap and delivered a smile. After he stopped to collect their points, which built toward free pitches, he put Rory's bat in the trunk.

"Can I use this bat at Little League practice and for games?"

"We'll have to see if the team supplies equipment, Rory." Seth waited while the boy buckled in before starting the car. "If you've watched Kemper at practice, does he use his bats?"

"Yeah, but his dad's always there telling Coach what to do. Even if Mom could go, she's too nice to do that."

"I wouldn't be too sure about that. Moms are fierce when it comes to their cubs."

"She's too busy to go to practice or a game. That's why we should go find the blue gems in the mine. Mom takes me sometimes and we leave flowers for my dad."

Seth had been trying to figure out what to say to deter Rory's interest in sapphires. "Rory, listen to me. I'm sorry you overheard my friend's phone call. It's rare for any gem hunter to make the amount of money Yoti mentioned. Not just rare, extremely rare. So forget any notion that it's an easy way to make money. It's not."

Rory fell silent. Seth glanced at him as he parked down from the café. To say the kid looked sullen would be putting it mildly. "Hey, buck up," Seth said. "Let's grab your stuff and find something to eat. Aren't you excited to tell your mom and grandmother how fantastic you did batting?"

"Did I really do good or are you saying that so I'll feel better?"

Seth exited the car and popped open the trunk. "Boy, for nine, you're cynical."

Rory hooked an arm through the strap of his backpack. "What's that mean?"

"'Cynical' is distrusting." Seth collected Rory's things and slammed the trunk lid. "You really batted well. I wouldn't have said that if you hadn't."

"Cool!" Rory sprinted to the door.

Entering behind him, Seth saw Rory head for the kitchen. Lila had apparently been on the lookout for them. She met her son with a grin and nodded often as he regaled her with his chatter.

Seth made his way to one of the few empty booths. The café was busy, and he thought Lila's face showed the strain of having worked a long day. He picked up a menu someone had left on the table. As he scanned it, he wished he could lighten her burden. He understood why Rory would feel the same.

Doreen came to the booth. Her arm remained in a sling, but she looked more relaxed than her daughter. "Tonight's special is spaghetti. My grandson seems keyed up. I hope you didn't fill his head with more claptrap about getting rich finding sapphires. I told Lila if you'd made close to that much you wouldn't waste your time hanging around Snowy Owl Crossing."

Seth bit back his first response. "Spaghetti sounds good. Your grandson had a successful trip to the batting cage. If everyone applauds his efforts, he'll return to baseball as his main interest."

She sashayed off. And Rory soon ran over and slid into the booth. "Mom said she has our game dates. She's gonna ask if Mrs. Watson can work that first afternoon."

"When is your first game?"

"Next Saturday."

Seth drummed his fingers on the table. "We should have Zeke's barn roof on by then. Now that school is out you and I can squeeze extra practice time around League practices."

"Will Coach let me play in the first game?"

Lila came to deliver their meals just as Seth opened his mouth to answer. "Yes, I need to know, too," she said, looking anxious. "It's not easy to get a relief cook for Saturday afternoons. I'd hope if I arrange time off that I can see Rory play."

"How much lead time do you need? I'll ask the coach his plans at their first practice. If I ran the show I'd play every kid in the first game to see their strengths and weaknesses. But I'm not in charge."

"By the way, the high school principal and his family were in earlier. You missed them by a few minutes. If you're still interested in the job we discussed last night…? Because I said something when he paid his check and he'd like to talk to you."

"Sure thing. Myra told me what I need to do to teach provisionally while I'd take classes online for a teaching credential."

A huge smile lit Lila's face and swept away the signs of stress that had concerned Seth. "We can talk later, if you're up for tea again," he said.

"Maybe. I need to cut out the fabric for the infant sleep sacks I plan to sell at the Thanksgiving bazaar. Jewell called Tawana today. She leaves Monday and has her pitch to the House Natural Resource Committee memorized."

Doreen called for Lila to check something in the oven. She rushed away in the same kind of whirlwind that had brought her to their booth.

Seth picked up his fork and dug into his spaghetti.

"Are you going to teach school?" Rory asked, swirling his fork in his noodles.

"I'm going to see what it'd take for me to teach science at the high school and coach some of their sports."

"Why?"

Breaking a chunk off his garlic bread, Seth debated launching a first salvo about his growing romantic interest in Lila. Unsure how to go about it, he took a different tack. "I like this town. My brother lives here. You and your mom live here. If I stay, I need to earn money."

"But…but…can't you go get the blue stones?"

"Rory, no. The mere suggestion upsets your mother. You understand how much it hurt her to lose your dad in the mine accident, don't you?"

"I guess. Everybody cried a long time. Mom still does when we go there to leave flowers. I don't think it looks scary or different from the land around our ranch."

"You weren't very old when it happened, Rory. It was probably scary for your mom. Eat now, before your spaghetti gets cold."

"Okay. If you teach high school, does that mean you can't help me get better at baseball?"

"The opposite. I'd have summers off."

The boy's tension dissipated and he began to eat.

SOME HOURS LATER at home, after Seth had taken Ghost for his nightly run and had a shower, he went online to read up on provisional teaching certificates. By the time he heard Lila and Rory arrive home, he thought it seemed doable.

Unlike the prior evening when he'd rushed downstairs, tonight he gave them time to complete their routine. The fishermen had long since retired.

The kitchen light was off when Seth descended. Thinking he'd waited too long and now wouldn't have any alone time with Lila struck a blow. Until he realized a light burned in the dining room.

Lila had printed flannel material spread out over the large table. Seth coughed to alert her as soon as he realized she had scissors in her hand.

She looked around and hailed him with a smile and wave of the sharp scissors. "I thought maybe roofing and Rory wore you out and you fell asleep early."

He walked up behind her, bracketed her narrow waist with his hands, bent and nuzzled her neck with his lips.

Lila relaxed and tipped her head to allow him greater access. "Hmm. You have a nice way of saying hello."

"I shouldn't interrupt your work. Your day's been as long as mine and perhaps more stressful."

"Will it go to your head if I say glimpsing you gives me a floating sensation?"

"No kidding?" Seth's hands tightened and he brought her closer for another nibble. "How do you always manage to smell like springtime, morning, noon or night?"

"You like my perfume? Kevin hated it. I stopped buying it for quite a while." She set down the scissors, turned in his grasp and initiated a solid kiss. "I don't have many indulgences," she admitted, dropping flat on her heels. "But I grew up loving the scent of magnolias. Now I buy this perfume for me."

"You'll have to write down the name and I'll gladly keep you supplied."

She let her hands drift down the front of his shirt. "I should get back to cutting out these patterns. You can pull up a chair and talk to me."

Seth let her go and went to the other side of the table. Otherwise he'd be too tempted to entice her away from work.

"Did Rory really bat well? He must've told me and Mom that fifty times after you left the café."

"He did. He follows directions and honestly has a lot of natural ability. It's hard for me to believe the coach never saw that."

"Do you think the coach will let him play in a game? Some kids might like the idea of being on the team. Rory will want to play."

"At this level, a coach should play every kid at least part of the game. If he doesn't, we'll find another team."

"Seth, this is Snowy Owl Crossing not Boston. There aren't a lot of choices here."

"True. He's going to be good enough to be chosen."

Lila shot him a huge smile. "You're good for us. And I have to thank you for getting Rory's mind back on baseball and off finding gems."

Seth shifted uncomfortably in the straight-backed chair. He was glad Rory hadn't returned to the subject with Lila. So maybe his last lecture had hit home. "Hey, I wanted to ask you if I should phone the high school to talk to the principal about that job. Or does the district hire? The website wasn't clear."

Lila folded and set aside material she'd cut out. "I think the principal interviews. You're really serious, then?"

Hearing the catch in Lila's voice, and seeing her quick exhale, Seth left his chair and circled to where she stood. Cupping her face in both hands, he said in total earnestness, "I've never been more serious about any decision I've made in my life. You fill a void I've never quite had filled. Just tell me I have a chance to make a difference for you. A positive difference," he said with feeling.

"You already do, but I keep thinking you're too good to be true. And I worry that something bad is going to drop out of the sky to wreck what we're building."

Seth kissed the tip of her nose. "You mean like the snowy owl sweeping down to take Rory's baseball? We're all too big for that, so quit worrying."

"I even like your quirky sense of humor, Mr. Maxwell."

Her cell phone rang. She picked it up off the table. "It's Mindy, one of the Artsy Ladies," she murmured. "I phoned her earlier. I should take this call."

Seth skimmed another kiss over her upturned mouth. "I'll feed the horses in the morning before I go to Zeke's. Batting practice with Rory again in the afternoon. Maybe tomorrow evening we can talk about how to snag a little alone time together."

Lila's eye roll spoke of the futility of that prospect.

Seth, though, wasn't easily deterred.

Chapter Nine

When Seth arrived at Zeke's to start installing the new metal roof, a gaggle of neighboring ranchers had showed up to help. They were nice guys who made Seth feel welcome. He soon learned this wasn't their first rodeo when it came to roofing barns. They gossiped and razzed one another throughout, but the project got done quicker than Seth and Zeke had thought. At noon the men's wives showed up with a potluck. Seth found himself missing Lila.

Missing her so acutely, he opted to skip lunch with the group and instead drove to the café. It was busy. Seth looked around for Rory since school had ended the day before. He went to the pass-through.

Lila spotted him when she set an order on the sill and came out. "This is a surprise. I thought you were roofing all day."

He explained the convergence of helpful neighbors. "With so many hands we finished early. Then the wives brought food. It turned into a couples party. I felt out of place. Nothing any of them said or did."

He zeroed in on Lila with longing. "I just wished you'd been there."

"It sounds as if it would've been fun," she said wistfully.

"I didn't bring it up to make you feel bad."

"I know. But if you hang with me you'll miss a lot of gatherings."

"I don't think so," he returned seriously. "But… I'm keeping you from work. Where's Rory today? I don't see him anywhere."

"He rode his bike to Kemper's. Since you've helped Rory play better ball, the boys are best friends again." She snapped her fingers. "That reminds me, I asked Sarah Jane Watson to work in my place the afternoon of their first game. It may be the only one I can attend, but I want to be there for Rory."

"Great. He'll be over the moon. Is he coming back here this afternoon before practice?"

"Could you get him at the Barneses' home? Mr. Barnes picked up the boys' uniforms."

"Give me their address. Since I have extra time I might drop by the high school and speak with Principal Morgan about the coaching job."

Lila took out her order pad, tore off a sheet and jotted down an address. "The high school is right on your way. I'm probably selfish, but I hope it works out."

Seth took the paper. "I hope so, too. Can you let Kemper's mom know I'll be there at three? And we'll show up back here for supper."

Lila ignored her mother, who twice slapped the

order bell. She walked to the door with Seth. "It seems I'm always thanking you. But no amount of thanks is enough. Even before Mom got hurt I wasn't sure how I'd get Rory to practice or games."

"Stop thanking me and just accept, okay? By the way, how's your mother doing?"

"Better. The doctor allowed her to remove the sling a couple of hours every day, so she insists on working."

"She's a tough lady. And she's watching us right now or I'd kiss you goodbye. When you're comfortable letting her and Rory know we've stepped our friendship up a level, I'm ready to oblige."

"Soon. It's most important that Rory be okay. I guess that'll depend on what you find out at the school. We can't kid ourselves, Seth. I know you need a job if you're going to stay in Snowy Owl Crossing."

"True. But I'm a man of many talents." He waggled his eyebrows and Lila's face turned a tad red before she shooed him out the door.

SETH'S UNSCHEDULED MEETING with the high school principal went very well. The man had heard of his baseball record and his geology degrees, which helped to the point that Morgan phoned a friend at the university who said she'd talk to Seth about what he'd need to secure a permanent job at the school. Morgan said to call him once he got transcripts, applied and received a provisional license. He gave Seth his home number and the number for his university friend.

When he got back to the bed-and-breakfast, the

fishermen were leaving. Seth knew they'd be replaced the next day by another group Lila said was also repeat customers.

He'd never been one to procrastinate, so he called and talked with the advisor. She suggested a summer class he could take once they got his transcripts, which Seth immediately registered for online. He ordered his transcripts, worrying that he hadn't studied in quite a while. But he saw this as a step closer to putting down roots and, Lord willing, getting closer to Lila. Until this minute he hadn't let himself think in terms of marriage. Now a full range of emotions tied to everything marriage meant flowed through him in a warm rush of pleasure.

He was so buoyed up he was bursting to tell someone. The only confidant available was Ghost. He rubbed the dog's belly and gave him fresh water, all while sharing his news. Seth laughed out loud on his way out to pick Rory up at the Barneses'. He pictured confessing all of this later to Lila.

The boys stood outside an elaborate dwelling Seth deduced had cost a mint. He'd never asked what Matt Barnes did for a living. Now he guessed he was a doctor or a lawyer.

Rory wheeled his bike to the back of Seth's rental car, which he realized was the next thing he needed to change.

"I got my uniform," Rory announced, pausing to wave to Kemper, who climbed into his dad's BMW.

"Your mom told me." Seth held up the shirt. "Badgers? Why not snowy owls?"

"The school teams are the fighting owls or white owls and stuff. Little League teams pick other animals."

"Makes sense. Hop in. Do you have to wear the uniform to practice?"

"Nope, only the cap. Can I keep the Yankees cap? I can wear it at home."

"It's yours." Seth shoved in a CD and soon whistled along.

"You're happy," Rory noted when the song ended.

"I am. I talked to the high school principal about coaching next year. And I got the ball rolling to fill out paperwork, get fingerprints and even take one class."

"So you're staying here? Kemper's dad said he bet you'd leave before winter."

Seth sought the boy in his rearview mirror. "Do you care either way?" Rory thought about his answer so long Seth began to sweat.

"I thought you'd change your mind and go to China for those red stones. I don't want you to go away, but your friend said you'd make lots of money. Money's important." Rory said it so seriously.

Seth eased out a breath. "He said someone else found the rubies. Maybe all the gems were already gone. Yoti hasn't called back to brag or anything."

"Oh. Kemper's dad is buying him a batting machine."

"Is that why you keep bringing up money?"

"No. Yes. I guess."

Seth pulled into the parking lot at the ball diamond. Some others were already there. He turned in his seat to check on Rory and saw him slumped and sour faced. "I'm sure it's hard when your best friend's folks buy him so much. But remember, you said you like your bat better than his costlier ones."

"But his mom and dad go to his practices and his games. My mom's gotta work all the time 'cause we never have enough money."

"Listen, I don't want to ruin the surprise, but she told me she's going to your first game."

"I knew that. But that's only one game, Seth. If we could find a bunch of those gemstones, she could be at home like Kemper's mom."

Seth rubbed the back of his neck. Maybe getting on the field to play would get Rory's mind off money. Ever since Yoti's phone call, the kid had been fixated on striking it rich.

The day's practice went well. Better for Rory than Seth dared hope. Coach Landis jogged up with his clipboard as they prepared to leave. "Maxwell, I have to tell you I've never seen a kid's batting improve as much in a few days as Rory's. Genius, man. Genius."

Seth set his hand atop Rory's wind-tossed red hair. "He gets the credit. Like I told his mother, he's got a lot of natural ability."

"I'm not sure there is such a thing. But if he keeps playing like he did today, he'll be starting in our first game with the Bears on Saturday. Did you get a game schedule?"

"Rory's mom has one."

"You guys live together? That may sound nosy, but it's important that I have a handle on what goes on in the lives of my players."

Seth had puffed up to tell the man what he could do with his question, but his explanation made sense. Only he shouldn't be so blunt about such stuff around a kid. "I rent from Rory's mom at the Owl's Nest. My twin brother owns the Flying Owl Ranch nearby. I'll be here all summer to help Rory and perhaps beyond. Count on that."

Seth said goodbye and carried Rory's net bag of equipment to his car.

"Do you like my mom?" Rory asked as he buckled his seat belt.

"Of course."

"Kemper said if you like my mom enough you might marry us."

Seth let the car lurch forward and quickly corrected it. "Do any of your classmates have stepparents?"

Rory made a funny face. "I don't know what that is. You mean like Hope Johnson's dad got sick last year and died? Mine, too, before I went to first grade. Hope lives with her mom, grandma and grandpa. I live with Mom, but Memaw sometimes checks my homework. Everyone else in my class got regular parents."

Feeling as though he'd stepped in over his head, Seth fell back on telling Rory his mom would be happy that Coach Landis said he'd play in Saturday's game.

"He said if I keep playing like I did today. What if I don't?"

"You will," Seth said with conviction. Then they both fell silent on the drive to the café.

Rory burst inside, bubbling over about his practice. Lila, Doreen and all the customers gave Rory high fives at his news that he'd made two base hits.

Lila gave Seth's waist a secret squeeze. "I've no idea how you worked such wonders. Don't deny it. Dale Landis made no secret that Rory wasn't playing well."

"Only because no one guided him. I have something to tell you about my visit to the high school. Can we talk after you get home?"

"Sure, but I may be late. I have rooms to ready for new guests and laundry from the ones who left."

"I could strip the beds and start the wash following my run."

"You'd do that?" Lila looked shocked.

"There's no limit to what I'd do for us to have more time alone," he said.

"Myra always talks about how much Zeke does to help her at the ranch. Our group thought she was exaggerating. Did you both get some recessive gene?"

Seth laughed. "Our parents both had jobs and they believed everyone who lived in the house had to pitch in to make it run."

"I wonder if I should expect more from Rory. He helps out here, but at home I let him be a kid."

"I've seen him feed Ghost and take him out. Zeke and I got a weekly allowance for doing chores. Some had to be saved. The rest we could spend however we liked."

"Hmm. There's not much for a kid to spend money on in a small town."

Seth might have suggested letting Rory pay for some time at the batting cage, but he didn't want Lila to take that as a hint to pay him back for the sessions. Her mom banged on the order bell and Lila took off. They didn't have another opportunity to talk.

It was 9:00 p.m. when Seth heard Lila bumping things around in a room down the hall. The noise jarred him out of reading material for his first class. He hadn't realized how engrossed he'd be in behavioral management. He'd made his application. Even if this class didn't count, he found it fascinating. Saving what he'd downloaded, he crossed to the door and tripped over Ghost, who he'd brought to his room and was now sleeping sprawled at the foot of Seth's bed.

The dog raised his head and yawned. Belatedly he climbed to his feet and followed Seth down the hall.

"Hey, you should have tapped on my door. I'd have come help make up beds."

Lila stopped plumping a pillow. "I saw the note that you'd taken Ghost. You didn't say where you took him."

"Sorry, I brought him to my room." He followed her across the hall with her next armload of sheets.

"I applied for provisional certification," he said,

going to the other side of the bed and signaling she should toss him half of the bottom fitted sheet.

"Seth, that's fabulous. So the job looks promising?"

"Mr. Morgan liked my background. He referred me to a university advisor. I figured trying to get back in the habit of studying would be a killer. But I dived right in. That's why I didn't come downstairs. Time got away."

They worked in tandem to tighten the top sheet and smooth on a clean spread.

"You helped me tremendously by having a load of sheets washed and dried and tossing the bedspreads in the washer. Now the rooms are ready for new customers, I have time to sew the sleep sacks I cut out last night." Lila motioned him out of the room.

Seth dropped an arm around her shoulders and Lila twined her fingers with his as they navigated the stairs. Ghost brought up the rear.

"Rory's all but made himself sick worrying whether Coach Landis will actually let him play in Saturday's game."

"He's a good player. He needs to stop being so anxious."

Lila paused in the lower hall and glanced up at him. "For worriers, that's easier said than done. Does nothing worry you?"

"Plenty." He captured her between his body and the dining room wall and, after bracketing her head with his hands, laid a row of kisses near her eye, her ear and finally her lips.

She clung to his neck and plastered her length

against him with the most sizzle they'd shared yet. "Wow," she mumbled when Seth finally lifted his head.

"Know what worries me? That I won't please you. That I can't make you happy. I have to muscle my way into your life, Lila. You're so competent on your own."

"You please me, Seth. If you can't see that, it's because part of me is afraid to be happy. I'm afraid everything will fall apart."

Seth gave her some space, but kept rubbing his thumbs over her soft cheeks. "We need to relax and take things day by day. Like going to Rory's game. With all the time you spend at the café, maybe eating out afterward isn't a big deal for you. But most players' families go celebrate. It's a chance for the three of us to let loose and spend time together. Kind of like the evening we all played catch."

"It sounds lovely. I'll try not to think about time lost on this sewing project."

"And I'll erase any need to study that day."

Smiling, they came together in another mutual kiss. This time Lila broke their connection. "Any more of this and I won't get any work done tonight."

Seth reluctantly stepped away. "I'll put Ghost up and make sure his doggy door is latched. Kissing you is infinitely more enjoyable, but I guess we should skip fixing tea and each get back to work, knowing we have fun time scheduled for Saturday."

Lila didn't agree quickly, but took a deep breath and finally nodded.

Saturday started out hectic. Seth had turned out the horses after feeding them and was putting fresh hay in the stalls when Rory bounded in, dressed in his game attire. It was barely 6:00 a.m. "Can we practice?" he shouted. "I know you said I played good at practice yesterday, but it's a long time till two o'clock."

"There'll be a warm-up at two, Rory. You don't want to strain your muscles. Does your mom know you're wearing your uniform already?"

"No. She's making breakfast. She said to change at Memaw's. Can I stay with you instead of going to the café? Maybe we should go to the batting cages."

Seth spread a last pitchfork full of hay and set it aside. "Let's go talk to your mom." He stripped off his gloves and tucked them into his back pocket.

"You look like a cowboy today." Rory's expression said he disapproved.

Eyeing the boy from beneath the brim of his summer straw hat, Seth decided it best to keep silent. "Let's go in the back door. My boots are dirty," he said.

"Didn't you buy team shirts for you and Mom to wear?"

"You know I did. I gave your mom hers last night. Rory, it's eight hours before we need to wear them. We don't want them to get dirty. Same with your uniform."

Lila heard the last comment as they entered the kitchen via the back door. "Rory, I said we'd take your uniform to the café. I'm sorry, Seth. He's bouncing off the walls."

"It won't always be like this," Seth promised. "This is his first game. It gets to be old hat."

"My hat's brand new," Rory exclaimed, making the adults laugh.

"Your mother said you don't approve of letting him play video games on my tablet. He wants to practice batting, but I don't want him worn out before the game. I have a pot load of applications to fill out. I can set up a video baseball game to keep him occupied until I pick you up this afternoon."

Lila set a second stack of pancakes on the warming tray. "Move, please, so I can take this to the dining room."

Seth started to relieve her of the heavy tray, but she jerked it away. "You smell like barn and you have hay on your shirt."

He pulled back fast.

"Mom's out of sorts today," Rory said. He started to cry. "I wanted today to be perfect."

Lila rushed back into the room and she and Seth bumped heads as both bent to console Rory. "Sorry, my mother's fussing because I'm leaving Sarah Jane to cook for the supper crowd by herself. I told you she can guilt me like no one else. And she disapproves of video games."

Seth straightened Rory's ball cap then he massaged Lila's tense shoulders. "Everyone take a deep breath. The café will survive and we'll have a great time cheering on Rory's team."

Blinking back her tears, Lila wiped Rory's face with

a tissue. "Seth's right. Take his tablet. My mother's being poopy."

That made Rory laugh out loud.

"I'll set up a baseball video game. I can't wait to start reading about how compromise deflects bad behavior."

"Really?"

"Really," Seth reiterated. "That class is gonna be worth every penny."

QUITE A FEW parents were in the bleachers by the time they got to the field. Doreen had kept finding things she wanted Lila to do until Lila called a halt and shooed Seth and Rory out the door. The smattering of early customers wished Rory good luck.

"I see Lori Barnes," Lila said. "Surely she didn't come without Kemper's dad."

"He's down with the team. Why don't you sit with her while I check a few things with the coach? The other dads are all on the field." Seth jerked around and stammered, "I—I'm not claiming to be Rory's dad."

"It's okay, Seth."

He fancied he heard enough wishful longing in Lila's short response that it gave him ideas. Then he was tugged away by Rory yanking on his hand, and he saw Zeke and Myra. They waved and met Lila in the bleachers. Seth felt better leaving Lila with family while he spoke with the coach. It wasn't that he had anything against Lori and Matt Barnes. But Zeke and Myra were going to join them after the game at an

Old West restaurant. Matt and Lori were more likely to end up at the country club.

Rory left Seth his equipment bag and ran off to join teammates. Seth walked up behind the coach as Matt Barnes said, "Landis, I want—no, given the fact I'm funding the soda cart, I *expect* Kemper to be team captain."

Seth cleared his throat to alert the men he was there.

Landis whirled. "I suppose you think Rory should be captain. He is my most improved player."

That revved Seth's heart, but he held up both hands. "He's happy getting to play. I would like to sit behind the kids for a while, though."

Landis nodded. Seth skirted the two men and called Rory over.

"Remember I said to pretend this is just another practice. Watch the ball and choose your plays."

Rory took his mitt. "Mom's sitting with Auntie Myra. Are you goin' up there or will you stay so I can talk to you?"

"I'll stay here for a bit. Give me five. You'll do great." They smacked hands and Seth was glad to see Rory loosen up.

By the second inning the Badgers were ahead two to one. Kemper popped out with a fly. Rory hit a line drive, but got tagged out at second base. He'd rotate at bat again in inning four. Seth left his seat and climbed up to sit with Lila.

"Zeke's been explaining the game," she said.

"When I went to school I just never watched sports. I hate that Rory didn't make a run."

"He'll make another. It's early." Seth took her hand and saw Myra nudge his brother.

Rory caught a high fly to retire the Bears. When he next came up to bat Lila practically cut off circulation to Seth's fingers. Rory hit a double, driving in a run. All the Badgers fans jumped up yelling.

"I don't know how much of this my heart can stand," Lila exclaimed, burying her face on Seth's shoulder as Rory slid but got thrown out at home.

Seth kissed her nose. "There are two innings to go, babe."

The score was tied. Zeke stood. "Seth, let's go buy sodas for everyone."

"Sure." Seth wasn't surprised that Zeke asked what his situation was with Lila once they were out of earshot.

"This isn't for publication, but I believe she's the woman I want long term in my life."

Zeke ordered the sodas, but didn't congratulate his twin. Instead he passed Seth two sodas and said, "Myra told me about the high school job and that you're signing up for college. Lila shared that with the other Artsy Ladies."

"So? Something's bugging you. Get it off your chest."

"You passed up an opportunity to make a lot of money playing pro baseball to hunt gems. Monday, Myra ran into Doreen at the doctor's. She said Rory overheard a call from one of your gem-hunting buds who asked you to meet him in China, where some dude made a fortune. Rory said on rubies."

"Right. I turned the opportunity down. But the very talk makes Lila nervous. I'll thank you to let the subject lie. I'm staying put."

"Okay, okay." Zeke led the way back to the women.

"You were gone through the whole inning," Myra said, popping the top on her cold drink. "Are you guys cool? It looked like you were arguing."

"We're cool," Seth said, passing Lila a soda.

In the fifth, Kemper struck out. His dad was not happy, especially when Rory hit a three-bagger and drove in two runs.

But the Bears were a seasoned team. They gained in the bottom of the fifth and the Badgers didn't score again. They lost the game by one run.

Seth went along congratulating all their players while Matt Barnes railed at the coach, insisting on a lineup change before next weekend's game against the Bobcats.

Corralling the family, Seth confirmed supper reservations with Zeke.

"Why are we celebrating?" Rory looked glum. "We lost."

Seth hoisted him up in his arms. "You kids played great for your first game of the season. The Bears got lucky today. Even the pros win some and lose some, slugger."

"They do." Rory grinned. "Mom, can I order a chocolate shake with my steak burger?"

"You may." She leaned close to Seth. "You got him past that disappointment."

At the restaurant they were seated at a large round table. The waiter asked Rory about the game, agreeing a one-run loss wasn't bad.

The four adults, who never got to go out, chatted and laughed throughout the meal. They parted ways promising to do it again.

Two minutes after Rory buckled up, he fell asleep.

Lila yawned and stretched. "I don't know when I've had a better time. I wish this day wasn't over."

"It doesn't have to be," Seth said quietly after making sure Rory still slept. "I don't know about you, but I'm ready to move our relationship into the realm of consenting adults. So you don't think it's spur of the moment, the other day when I stopped to make tonight's reservation, I spotted a drugstore. I went in and bought protection," he murmured.

Lila blinked at him like one of the snowy owls.

"There's no pressure. My door will be unlocked. There's no one else, and hasn't been for a long time. If it turns out it's not the right time for you, okay. Condoms keep."

"Shh!" She shot out a hand to grip his arm as she glanced again at her sleeping son. "I… I… I…"

"Lila, honey, I understand if our making love has never entered your mind."

"It has." She sounded strangled. "But there's a big gap between thinking and doing."

At her confession, heat surged to his lower abdomen. He turned down the lane to the ranch, glad he'd laid his heart on the table whether or not this was the night.

Because Lila woke Rory up to walk into the house instead of asking him to carry the sleeping kid inside, Seth felt that was her answer.

Almost an hour later he sat on his bed in his shorts, trying to commit to memory dry information on the foundations of education. He thought he heard a light tap on his door. He set aside his laptop and got up in time to see the door slowly open. Lila peeked in then took her sweet time running her gaze the length of his barely clothed body.

"Hmm," she murmured, closing the door with her bare foot at the same time she untied her summer robe and let it drop to the floor behind her. The bed lamp shone through her short, gossamer nightie.

Seth's mouth went bone-dry and, for a second, he thought his heart had stopped. Until it began to pound in his ears louder than a bass drum.

"Could we have less light?" Lila requested. "And if you don't quit standing there and come touch me, I'm either going to fall apart or turn tail and run."

Seth moved as fast as he'd ever moved. He cut the lamp to its glowing base. With lightning speed he shut down his computer, claimed the condom box he'd tossed in the nightstand drawer, swept Lila up and tumbled them both into his generous bed.

His first kiss tracked from her lips down her warm neck to stop as he savored one of her breasts through the thin fabric and then moved to lavish the same attention on the other one.

She wrapped her legs around Seth's hips. In a voice far from steady, she said against his mouth as it again found hers, "I don't have all night. I wish I did."

"We're not going to rush," he whispered huskily. "I intend for our first time to be memorable. To leave you satisfied yet wanting more." And he kissed his way down to the heart of her femininity.

Fireworks flashed behind her eyes as Seth shed his shorts a moment before handing her a condom. Thoughts that had crossed her mind mere weeks after meeting him welled up. She need look no further to find a man who cared enough to put her needs and desires first.

Chapter Ten

Lila and Seth's stolen night of lovemaking transformed their relationship. She knew it. Felt it. Changes were subtle at first, but over the next several weeks they found ways to spend more time together and they talked about their future. Still they'd only managed one additional night in each other's arms.

Lila hadn't thought her newfound happiness showed until she and her mom were alone in the café kitchen one morning and Doreen pounced. "That man you continue to make goo-goo eyes at and moon over doesn't even have a paying job. What kind of man is content to live off a woman even if he hangs around feeding her horses? A sad role model for Rory, that's who."

Lila straightened from loading the dishwasher with breakfast dishes. "If you mean Seth, he's signed up for online college courses to be able to teach at the high school next fall. And for your information, he returned his rental car and bought a king-cab pickup. Plus he continues to pay his rent on time. He's not living off of me, Mother."

Doreen slammed pots around. Mother and daughter glared at one another until Rory, who'd been watching TV in his memaw's apartment, ran down the stairs and exploded into the room. "Mom, Mom, can I ride my bike to Kemper's? His dad got his batting machine set up. Kemper 'vited me over to try it out."

"You have a makeup game this afternoon. Seth plans to pick you up here at one. That's only two hours away, and you boys shouldn't get tired out."

"We won't. I can call and ask Seth to pick me up at Kemper's."

"He's studying and may not have his phone turned on."

"Then when he comes, send him there. Please, Mom. Kemper's got his own batting machine. I want one so bad. I bet if Seth marries us he'll buy me one."

Doreen choked and Lila's jaw dropped. "Rory, what…where in heaven's name did you get that notion?"

"I saw you guys kissing. Kemper said that's what moms and dads do. And one day me 'n Seth were talking. He asked if I knew what a stepdad was. All the kids on the team think he is my dad."

"Seth and I haven't actually discussed marriage per se," Lila said mostly for her mother's benefit. "And Lori Barnes told me what that machine cost, young man. As a teacher, even if he coaches, Seth will never earn what Kemper's dad does as a lawyer. So get that nonsense out of your head. Yes, you may go to Kemper's. I want a word with Seth, so I'll direct him your way when he comes to pick you up."

The boy stuffed his hands in his pockets. “Is he gonna be mad at me like you are?”

“I’m not mad.” Lila adjusted the net holding her hair. She did think if Seth contemplated marriage, she ought to hear of it first.

With Wild Horse Stampede folks starting to arrive in Wolf Point, the café’s lunch and supper crowd had already mushroomed. Doreen’s sling had been removed, but Lila still handled most of the cooking. Her mom and Becky waitressed and cleared tables. Lila soon got so busy she forgot to fuss over Seth.

The place hadn’t slowed down one iota when he arrived at ten to one.

Doreen accosted him as he walked in. “You’re in big trouble. But Lila’s too busy to yell at you now. Rory’s at Kemper’s. You need to pick him up there for the game.”

Seth’s head wasn’t fully out of his studies, but he couldn’t think why Lila would be upset with him. Ignoring Doreen, he poked his head in the kitchen. “Doreen said Rory’s at Kemper’s. She also said you’re PO’d at me.”

“I’m not mad at you. It’s something Rory said. We’ll have to talk later. I’m swamped with orders.”

“Okay. We’ll drop by here after the game. I wish you could go.”

“Me, too.” Lila waved a hand helplessly toward a full order carousel.

Seth walked over and kissed her. “I hope that makes things better.” He didn’t care that Doreen saw and scowled as he brushed past her and went out.

He racked his brain to think what Rory could've said. He hoped it wasn't anything about hunting for sapphires or rubies. He thought he'd put that to rest once and for all.

Driving down the Barneses' block he saw Lori getting into a BMW that matched Matt's. Rory stood at the curb with his bike. Was Lori leaving Rory alone? Surely not. Compared to everyone else he'd met in Snowy Owl Crossing, Matt and Lori Barnes were the most preoccupied with themselves. Case in point, she backed out and drove off without waving. Kemper, however, did.

Seth pulled to the curb, let the pickup idle and got out to put Rory's bike under the canopy.

"Are you mad at me?" It was Rory's first question after Seth slid back behind the steering wheel.

"Should I be? Your grandmother seems to think I'd done something wrong, but your mom was too busy to talk. How about if you clue me in?"

The boy picked at his fingers. "Kemper got a batting machine. I told Mom if you married us I bet you'd buy me one. She and Memaw had a cow, 'specially after I said I saw you guys kissing. Or maybe it was when I said you asked if I knew what a stepdad was." He shrugged.

"That was some conversation. Don't fret about it. Your mother and I will iron things out. You do your best today, okay? It's good we're getting this makeup game out of the way. According to the TV weatherman, we may be in for a big rainstorm."

"When? Rodeo's soon. It's always hot for that."

"Is that why the coach said there will be practices at the school but no game until Tuesday after next? I figured the switch took into account Independence Day."

"Yep."

"Gosh, I haven't been to a rodeo in years. Maybe your mom can get away and we'll all go."

"Nah, the café is always super busy. Auntie Jewell took me. She does veterinarian stuff there. Rodeo's okay, but not as fun as baseball. I guess we can go if you want. Mom said Auntie Jewell's gone somewhere to talk about the snowy owls. I heard Mom on the phone with Auntie Tawana."

"Is she well? I haven't heard your mom mention her craft group in a while."

"She's better, but behind on her job."

"Glad she's improved enough to be back at work. Well, here we are. Grab your equipment bag. I see you have grass stains on your uniform knees. Are you hurt?"

"Naw. I fell down at Kemper's. His machine spit out a really low ball. I tried to stop it from going past me. His machine does a lot of change-up pitches. It's fun."

Their talk fell off. Most of the other players were already warming up. Rory pulled out his mitt as Seth paused to get the batting order from Coach Landis. Since he was the only person there to cheer for Rory, he took a seat in the bleachers directly behind him.

The coin toss gave the Badgers first bat. Seth finished giving Rory the usual pep talk and he'd leaned back to watch when someone sat beside him and tapped his arm.

"Hey, Myra. I didn't know you were coming. Is Zeke here?" Seth craned his neck, looking around.

"No, but you received a couple of official-looking letters. Zeke thought I should run them over. One is from the Superintendent of Public Instruction. The other's from the Montana Department of Environmental Reclamation Projects. Zeke said maybe it has to do with one of your classes."

Seth took the letter from the superintendent and ripped it open. "Ah, this says they received my university transcripts and someone will post them to my file. Once that's done I'll be cleared to get a provisional teaching certificate. This is great." He folded it, stuck it in his back pocket and then tore into the second envelope. "Oh, wow, it's the permit to hunt for sapphires at the Opportunity Mine. So much has changed I forgot about this. I won't need it now, of course." He folded that letter, too.

"So, you've totally dropped gem hunting?"

"Yep. I'm thinking of asking a guy I know if he wants my quality equipment. I bought a few items here. Flashlights, ropes, a headlamp. They're stored in a chest in Lila's barn. If he doesn't want the stuff, maybe I can sell it online."

"Or hang on to them to see if teaching and coaching works out."

"It's going to work out, Myra."

A whistle blew and the game began.

By inning five the wind kicked up. Angry clouds

rolled overhead. Myra said to Seth, "I don't like the look of this weather. I hate to leave early, but I should go home and help Zeke check stock in our summer pastures. Some cattle freak at thunder and trample fences."

"I appreciate you bringing me the mail. Next time, call. I'll come pick it up."

Rory came back to the bench to sit directly in front of Seth again. Myra leaned down and apologized to him for not staying. "If you keep hitting like you've done up to now, the Badgers will win."

"Thanks, Auntie Myra. I hope it doesn't rain. Kemper said playing is awful when the diamond gets muddy."

"Maybe the rain will pass us by," Seth said. "Or hold off until tomorrow."

"Do we still gotta practice?"

The boy seated beside Rory spoke up. "If it only rains a little, yeah. Coach will cancel practice if there's lightning."

Seth stored that tidbit. The storm might double down or it could blow over.

The Badgers did win, and Rory drove in the winning run, although he got put out at third. It was the team's first victory and all the kids whooped and hollered.

Rory remained pumped on the drive to the café. He jumped out and ran inside ahead of Seth, telling everyone in earshot about the win. "Mom," he shouted at the kitchen door, "you shoulda been there. I batted real good. Coach said every player needs to spend time in a batting cage. We have enough room in the backyard for one." He sent a guilty look at Seth, who'd sauntered in behind him.

"I'll leave you to calm him down," Seth told Lila. "I think I'll go home and read up more on what courses I need next semester. I'll take his bike."

"Fine. Can you set it in the barn? A customer said it's slated to pour. To give you more study time Rory can come here tomorrow whether or not there's practice."

"Mom, I wanna go to Kemper's again. If we can't bat, we can play his new computer LEGO game."

"I suppose. Unless it rains too hard for you to ride your bike there. You know how busy we are with rodeo people."

"You're always busy." Rory kicked at a cabinet. "When can you ever do stuff like Kemper's mom?"

Seth set his hand on Rory's shoulder. "Apologize, slugger. Your mom works hard to keep you fed and clothed."

"Sorry," he mumbled.

Seth brushed a light kiss across Lila's furrowed brow. "Things will get better." Again he passed Doreen. This time he noticed she didn't look so sour.

IN THE MORNING the sky remained dark and overcast, but no rain had fallen so Seth turned the horses into the corral. The last of the fishermen had been replaced by two rodeo couples.

"This is my first summer in Montana," one of the rodeo goers said. "The weather channel's calling for rain."

The couples left and Seth returned to the barn. He saw Rory hooking his ball bag over his bike handle. "Hey, need some help? Maybe you should leave your bike here. It's probably going to rain hardest this morning. If it clears up for practice, I'll pick you up at the café."

"I asked Mom and I'm gonna go to Kemper's, anyway. I don't need any help. I'll put this in the Jeep by myself."

Maybe his mom had lectured him about taking more responsibility. Or perhaps the two had had a tiff at breakfast. Rory was acting a bit odd. Seth headed inside, intending to ask Lila, but she wasn't anywhere around. Ghost had already been fed. Seth felt bad he had missed a chance to smooch with Lila. Passing through to the dining room, he helped himself to a plate of breakfast burritos and went upstairs to cram before an online quiz.

He heard Lila start the Jeep, got up and went to the window. She was fast disappearing down the lane, and he realized she'd gotten a late start.

"RORY, DID YOU see Seth this morning?"

The boy jerked upright. "Yeah. He turned the horses out into the corral and talked to the rodeo guests. Why?"

"No reason. I missed seeing him this morning. I think he's anxious about his quiz."

"I don't like them or tests. Why does he hafta go to school? I didn't think adults had to study."

"He's changing jobs. He went to college, but not to teach."

"Did he have to go to school to hunt for gems?"

Lila shot Rory a sidelong glance. "He said his degrees are in geology. That's the science of the earth, rocks and minerals, I think."

"My teacher said our whole planet is layers of sand and rocks."

Lila smiled. "I'm happy you remember things your teacher tells you."

"Well, yeah. But every year they make us learn more. What did you take in college?"

"I didn't. I got married right out of high school. We bought the Owl's Nest and then I had you. I learned about cooking and homemaking from Memaw."

"Why doesn't Kemper's mom work?"

"Mr. Barnes has a high-paying job. A safe job," she added, making her son frown at her. "That's what I want for you, Rory, so study hard."

"Maybe I'll play pro baseball."

"Maybe," Lila agreed, parking outside the café. In moments her work swung into high gear and Rory trudged upstairs to watch TV until almost noon, when he came down again, begging to go to Kemper's.

"What's the weather like?" Lila asked as she flipped four burgers.

"I'll go look," he said as Becky walked into the kitchen.

She said, "The clouds are gray. But unless it's raining in the hills, the weather guys guessed wrong again. I'm sure that'll make the stampede promoters ecstatic. So, Rory, is Jewell taking you to see the bull riding again this year?"

Rory hiked his shoulders up to his ears.

Lila assembled burgers and dumped sizzling fries on four plates. She set them on the pass-through counter and hit the bell. "Jewell hasn't said if she's the backup vet for the rodeo this year. She's due home from DC soon. She called Tawana. I understand her meeting with the Natural Resource Committee didn't go as well as she'd hoped. We probably all need to give her space when she gets home."

"Mom, is it okay if I go to Kemper's?"

"I guess. Let me know if there's going to be ball practice so I can tell Seth."

He dashed off.

"I didn't hear him say yay or nay," Becky said, taking off her jacket to trade it for an apron.

"He's consumed with that stupid batting machine Matt Barnes bought Kemper. Seth said they cost more than a horse," Lila grumbled, whirling the order carousel to read the new slips her mother had clipped on.

"I'll go relieve Doreen. Maybe things will slow down by one so you can take a break, Lila."

"Dream on. More people come to the rodeo every year. But I can't complain. They bring tourism dollars to us."

The crowd thinned shortly before one. Doreen bustled into the kitchen. "Lila, I just took a phone call from Mrs. Landis. She said it's starting to thunder, so her husband canceled ball practice."

Lila looked up from scraping the grill. "The kids

will be disappointed. Rory's been at Kemper's for over two hours. If you and Becky can handle things for a while, I'll go get him. I don't want him riding his bike in this weather."

"That's wise," Doreen said, watching Lila strip off her apron.

Stuffing her hairnet in her jeans' pocket, she paused at the door. "If Seth phones or comes in, give him Mrs. Landis's message."

"Don't you suppose someone notified him?"

"He had an online quiz at ten thirty, and after that a Skype appointment with his college advisor. I'm not sure how long that'd take. I figure his phone's on vibrate, but he might not hear it if he got too involved."

"Okay. But you aren't going to be gone very long."

Lila left the café, seeing it had begun to spit rain. She saw lightning in the distance. As she drove the familiar route to the Barneses' house, she mulled over what she had to do to get her mother to accept that Seth meant a lot to her.

Rain pelted harder. Lila hadn't worn a jacket and her uniform got splotched with raindrops on her way to the Barneses' front door.

Kemper opened it when she rang the bell. He gaped at her for a long moment. "Mrs. Jenkins. What are you doing here?"

"I came to get Rory. I guess you know they've canceled practice."

"Yeah. But he left before Coach called."

"Left?" Lila rubbed her upper arms. Hadn't she driven the route he would've taken on his bike?

"Uh-huh. He went to go get the sapphires. From the mine," Kemper said, acting as if Lila ought to know.

Her heart began to pound. "Mi-mine?" she stuttered. "Kemper, I don't understand. He wouldn't ride his bike all the way out to the mine, alone, and when it was about to storm."

"I dunno. That's what he said. He said he got a flashlight and ropes from Seth."

Lila flew off the porch. She plunged down the slick sidewalk to her Jeep. Hands shaking, she took out her phone and called Seth.

The phone rang and rang on his end, but he didn't pick up. Twice she almost dropped her cell because she was trembling so hard. Finally she threw it on the passenger seat. She could drive to the mine, but it was closer to go to the ranch. Was this some scheme Rory and Seth had cooked up? After all of his pretty promises and all she thought they'd come to mean to each other, why would Seth go back on his word?

After two attempts she started the Jeep. *What had Seth promised?* Digging back through muddled memories, she recalled him saying it took a permit to hunt sapphires. Conceivably he could be turned down to teach even after obtaining provisional certification. Even if he had elected to go after sapphires to sell, why, why, why would he involve Rory?

Lila knew she shouldn't drive and use her phone, but she spared a moment to call the café. "Becky? It's Lila. No, don't get Mom. Give her a message. Tell her I hope you two can handle customers for a while.

Rory left Kemper's. He's not at the café by chance, is he?" She prayed the answer was yes and her churning stomach was all for naught.

"No, he isn't here. You sound upset, Lila. Is everything all right?"

"I'll let you know. I'm going home to see if Seth picked him up at Kemper's and he's wrong about saying Rory rode off on his own. Listen, Becky. I can't talk and drive. I'll check back later."

She took the corner off the highway to her lane on two wheels. The jolt reminded her of the time she'd put the Jeep in the ditch. The first time Seth had come to her rescue. The first time she'd started falling for his helpful ways.

Slowing, she strained to see through rain that suddenly hammered her windshield, hoping against hope to see Rory's bike. She did see Seth's new pickup. What did that mean? And there he was leading a horse into the barn.

Braking hard, she unbuckled and threw herself out. "Seth, Seth," she yelled.

He turned, left Merlin in the door to the barn and met Lila at the fence. "What is it, babe? Why are you home at this hour? Did something happen to your mom?" He dug out his phone. "Dang, I missed several calls. I had it on mute instead of vibrate."

"Seth, stop talking and listen to me." Her voice rose and fell frantically. "Did you give Rory a flashlight and ropes so he could go to the mine to look for sapphires? Of course you didn't," she muttered, registering his shocked expression. "I'm a nervous wreck. Kemper said Rory left his house early to ride his bike to the mine. He said Rory got a flashlight and ropes from you."

"He didn't. This makes no sense. But if he went to the mine, we need to go there fast. Wait, I stored some equipment in the barn. Come to think of it, Rory was there this morning with his ball bag."

"Get what you need. I know a shortcut. I'll drive."

SETH DIDN'T ADMIT to having ridden out there once himself. If it upset Lila more, she might not be able to drive.

He dashed into the barn, put Merlin in his stall and threw the tool chest open. He removed a head-lamp, oxygen tank and face mask. A big flashlight and ropes were gone. Wishing he was wearing sneakers instead of his new, slick-soled cowboy boots, he grabbed a horse lunge line from a wall peg and went out to toss everything in the backseat of the Cherokee. "Are you sure you're okay to drive, babe? Your hands aren't real steady."

"I have to be fine. What is all that gear you put in the back? Was that an oxygen tank?"

"Sometimes air in abandoned mines gets stale." He didn't say sometimes a mine produced toxic fumes.

"What possessed him?"

Seth huffed out a breath. "Yesterday Myra came to the game and brought my mail. I set them up as a forwarding address before I got here. One letter was a permit to explore the mine. She asked questions. I told her I had no intention of using it. Maybe Rory overheard us. I can't remember if he sat in front of us. Honestly his getting it into his head to go there is nothing I'd have imagined."

"I'm furious at you. Oh, I may throw up. My dad died in a mine. Kevin died in this mine. Seth…" Her fingers tightened and turned white around the steering wheel.

"Pull over. I'll drive."

She shook her head. "It's better that I have a task." She turned off the highway onto muddy tracks. "This is a fire road. It cuts driving time in half."

Seth cracked his window open. The rain—or Lila's anger—had steamed up the interior. He recognized the mine entrance the minute she slammed on the brakes. "Look," she said, her voice cracking. "There's his bike. I prayed we'd beat him here."

She started to open her door, but Seth caught her arm. "I want you to stay in the Jeep." Reaching back, he nabbed the equipment and quickly donned the hard hat with the headlamp. In seconds he'd strapped on the oxygen tank, but left the face mask hanging free.

"Waiting will drive me crazy," she said. "You need oxygen? Is the mine air bad? I should go with you."

"No. The air may be fine, Lila." Seth bracketed her chin in one hand. "Stay. Don't make me worry about you and Rory." He ran a finger over her lips. The bulky headlamp kept him from kissing her.

Coiling the long rope, he slung it over a shoulder and lurched out into the rain.

Inside the dark opening Seth took a minute to slow his heart rate and get his bearings. Speed mattered, but so did taking care. His headlamp illuminated the cavern. If he called Rory now he'd only get echoes. That day at the library he had studied a drawing the last gem hunter in here had sketched. But that library trip was weeks ago and fear rendered his memory fuzzy.

Venturing farther in, he recalled how the mine split. Snapping the headlamp on high beam, he saw both tunnels had rusty trolley tracks. Ore cars would have brought metal to this junction, where the tracks converged and ore went out to be dumped into trucks.

The right-hand tunnel had been the site of the cave-in. It had partially closed the left one, too, but much deeper down.

Reaching the juncture, Seth hollered for Rory. The boy's name rebounded, mocking him until the sound petered out. For the first time in all of his underground excursions, his belly cramped as he pictured Lila's anguish if he failed to find her son. Or worse, if he found him broken at the bottom of a shaft. Or… no, Seth erased the worst thought.

He chose the center shaft. A kid who was right-handed might automatically turn right. But if he held a flashlight in front of him, its arc wouldn't penetrate that far. Choice made, Seth descended rapidly, sticking to the rails, watching for rickety supports or broken beams. Every few feet he called out to Rory.

Although he worried the kid may have succumbed to the kind of bad air typically found deeper in a mine, Seth held off donning his oxygen mask so he could yell. His headlamp didn't reach far into the pitch blackness. Thinking he should see Rory's light, he considered turning back to check the other tunnel. As he hesitated, he imagined he heard a faint call. He rushed forward, but all at once the rails bent sharply around a corner. Seth slipped on a round rock and almost fell into a side shaft of the type often used to follow a productive vein. He caught himself and even as he teetered on the edge of a hole, he heard soft cries from below.

He tore off the cumbersome oxygen tank and lay flat, calling again.

"Daddy? Daddy!" The plaintive response drifted aloft, sending chills up Seth's spine. And making him fervently wish he was Rory's dad.

"It's Seth, Rory. Are you hurt?"

"Yes." Sniffles and then a thin "My left arm hurts bad. Help me. I can't get out."

Further frustrated because his headlamp outlined two adjacent shafts that hadn't been identified in the mine schematics, Seth cupped hands around his mouth and yelled down one. A distinct "Seth, help me!" rose from the other. That crudely dug shaft was likely the work of gem hunters. Maybe it wouldn't go down as far.

"Hold on, slugger. I'm coming to get you. It may take me a minute."

"Seth? Seth, where are you? Have you found Rory?" Lila's voice sounded high-pitched and distraught, drifting toward him from the main cavern.

Seth spun. His stomach balled tighter as his light bounced off rock walls shored up with wood. "Lila?

I found him," he yelled. "Please, sweetheart, don't come any farther. I'll get him and come back out to you. Stay in the main grotto."

"I ca-can't leave. My cell phone light gave out. Seth, I'm afraid. It's dark. Is Rory okay?"

Her voice sounded hollow as it echoed inside the chamber.

"He's talking," Seth shouted. "I'm going silent while I climb down to him. Stay where you are."

As quickly as unsteady hands allowed, he fashioned knots in the lunge line, thanking his lucky stars that it was long and tightly woven. He chose the most solid-looking beam and double looped the line around it, letting it dangle into the shaft. All the while Rory's cries unnerved him.

He tested the line and it held his weight. Hoping his nightly runs had kept him from going soft, Seth began a hand-over-hand descent. The slick leather of his boots hampered him. He should have removed them.

His headlamp revealed the shaft widening, not growing smaller. The hole went deeper than his light would penetrate. When with a bump he reached Rory he began to sweat. The boy perched on a broken four-by-four scaffold. His eyes were big, his face dirty. The large flashlight hanging from a cord around his neck put out feeble light. He clutched something in his right hand. Seth couldn't see what. His left arm looked swollen and oddly angled. Seth judged it broken, but he had nothing with which to bind it, supposing he managed to balance on the narrower crossbeam to effect this rescue at all.

His first try, his foot slipped, knocking a rock off. It fell a long time before he heard it hit bottom. The boots had to go. It took contortions, but he scraped them off and sent them into the abyss all while talking a stream of nonsense to the scared kid.

"Did you climb down here?"

"I fell. I saw this sparkly white rock. Maybe it's diamonds." Rory sniffled loudly.

"Maybe. Listen, Rory, it won't be easy for me to get us to the top. We each have on a belt. I'm going to get rid of your flashlight and buckle us together. Can you do exactly as I say even if it hurts?"

"Y-ye-yes," he stuttered. "I cried when I fell. My da-daddy said to not move until someone came, no matter if I got cold." He snuffled louder.

"That's good," Seth said, dropping the heavy flashlight. "Wait…your daddy?"

"Uh-huh, I remember…he was the only one who called me his little buddy. I heard him say, 'Little buddy, don't move. Someone will come.' And you did."

That sent shivers up Seth's spine. He was barely able to buckle them together and hug Rory awkwardly to his chest, knowing the sharp sob meant he'd caused him pain. Exerting every ounce of strength, relying on faith and all he'd learned roping up and down Afghanistan's cliffs in search of lapis, Seth began inching upward knot by knot.

Time seemed endless. Once both his stockinged

feet slipped off a knot. Rory screamed and Seth's heart slammed erratically. He dared not pause long. Hauling in a deep breath, he kept climbing and at long last he felt the cooler air in the upper mine sweep sweat off his brow. But he couldn't let down his hand-over-hand ascent until he felt Rory's backside and his own knees crest the rim of the hole.

He let go of the line and, although his hands burned, he unbuckled their belts. Even if he'd like nothing more than to curl into a fetal position the way Rory had, Seth remained aware of Lila somewhere out there in a black cave. Lila, who had reason to fear and hate mines in the worst way.

"Rory, I'm going to strip off my T-shirt and hope it's long enough to bind your arm so it won't hurt as much while I carry you out. Your mom's waiting in the main grotto. She's worried sick."

"Seth, I'm sorry I came. I didn't see any sapphires. I wanted a batting machine like Kemper's." His sobs increased as Seth molded the soft shirt material around the injured arm and across the kid's narrow chest.

"Shh. There'll be time to talk after we get out of here." He left the oxygen mask and tank he'd dropped earlier behind and hoisted Rory. Loose ore cut his feet through the thin material of his socks as he picked his way along the old rails. He hobbled the last twenty feet to where his headlamp illuminated a sight he'd prayed every step of the way to see.

Though Lila stood looking disheveled, wringing

her hands, with tears streaming down her pretty face, to Seth she was beautiful. A goddess. *His* goddess.

She raised her arms, no doubt to take her son, but Seth stumbled into them and with breath coming in spurts, he kissed her, pouring out every shred of his soul.

"Rory needs the ER," he rasped. "Let's get out of here."

Chapter Eleven

"Mama, are you mad?" Rory's chest shuddered in and out.

"No, honey, Mama loves you. What hurts? Did you fall?" Lila blinked in the daylight as they left the mine. It was no longer raining.

Rory tucked his dirty red hair under Seth's chin. "Uh-huh." He opened his right hand, in which he clutched a big white stone that sparkled in the natural light. "I saw this and thought it was a diamond. I bent over to grab it and fell in a hole. I can't move my left arm, Mama." He started to sob. "I bet I can't play baseball."

"Hon, the doctor will fix your arm. Seth, can you buckle him in beside you if I drive to the hospital?" Glancing back at him, she gasped. "Mercy, I saw what you did with your shirt, but where in the world are your boots? They were new."

"They're at the bottom of the shaft where I found Rory. It's a long story. One better saved till later," he said wearily. "Now my socks are getting wet."

"It still smells like rain, but thankfully the storm

has passed," she said, rushing ahead to unlock the Cherokee.

Directly above the car, a pair of snowy owls flew by, then made a large arc and circled back to disappear in a layer of low-hanging clouds.

"Wow, did you see that?" Lila gaped after them. "Tawana would say seeing them now signifies good luck."

Seth nodded. "I only drove out here one other time weeks ago. I saw owls that day, too. Maybe they nest in the mine. Are they like bats?"

"According to Jewell they took over abandoned eagle nests, or she's found them nesting atop boulders in the woods," she said, hurrying around to open his door. "People say they're good luck, and we all came out of the mine alive."

"True. Lila, I know Rory should be buckled in, but I'll hold him on my lap to keep his arm from jiggling when we travel this bumpy road."

She bit her lip, watching him awkwardly crawl into the backseat with her crying son. Rounding the hood, Lila got in. After twice stabbing the key at the ignition, she managed to start the car.

Seth darted a concerned frown in her direction while settling Rory, who yelped in pain. "Are you okay to drive? If not, I can probably manage."

"As bloody as your socks are, no way," she said and stepped on the gas.

Sinking into the seat, Seth allowed himself a relieved sigh. Every bone, every muscle, in his body ached and the bottoms of his feet stung like hell. But they were all together. Injuries were minor considering how much worse things might have been.

"Darn, I forgot to phone Mom. I called once to tell her why I didn't get back to the café. She's a bigger worrywart than me. She'll be in a tizzy."

"Let's get Rory to a doctor then worry about Doreen."

"And you," Lila said. "You'll probably need a tetanus shot. That's not all blood on your socks," she murmured, glancing back to where he'd stretched out his long legs along the seat. "Some spots look like rust. Everything in the mine is old."

"Did you hear that, Rory? I may need a big ol' shot," Seth said to distract him.

"I hope I don't," the boy said between hiccups.

They all quit talking, and it wasn't long before Lila pulled up in front of the emergency entrance. "If you'll take Rory and check in, I'll park. Oh, drat, my phone died or I'd call Mom."

"Take mine." Seth handed it off, slid out and, half hobbling, carried Rory into the building.

Surprisingly the ER wasn't too busy. Doreen had told Seth the morning he'd brought her in that in their small town the ER, lab and X-ray also served local doctors in private practice.

A nurse placed Rory and Seth on adjoining beds with only a curtain between. That would make it easier for Lila to keep an eye on both once she joined them.

Things moved fast. The doctor came and after a quick check of Rory's arm, ordered X-rays. It wasn't long before he had the images and asked a nurse to prepare cast material.

Lila stepped around Seth's curtain. "They're going to cast Rory's broken arm." Worriedly she lowered her voice. "I asked Dr. Rice to check him for a concussion. Rory… Rory said, oh it's foolish, but he said after he fell in a deep hole, Kevin told him not to move until someone came. I corrected him and said it was you. I mean, he knows his father died. Rory insisted it was before you came and only his daddy called him 'little buddy.' But that's impossible."

Seth shifted on the bed, taking Lila's hand. "He told me the same thing when I reached him. Lila…the first gem hunters left the mine after a day even though they found sapphires. Did you know they claimed the mine was haunted?"

"I heard rumors. Surely you don't believe that."

"Traveling in remote lands, I've witnessed odd miracles. Is it so hard to believe in guardian angels, sweetheart? Especially since all of you consider seeing snowy owls a good omen?"

She shrugged. "It won't hurt to have him checked for a head injury."

"No." Seth brought her hand to his lips for a kiss.

Lila bent toward him as if to kiss him on the mouth when the outer curtain was swept aside and a nurse shoved a gurney into the room. She ground to a halt, opened a chart and stared at Lila and Seth. "Mrs. Maxwell?"

Seth raised up on an elbow. "I'm Mr. Maxwell."

"This is my second day working here. Are you Zeke and Myra Maxwell?"

Lila straightened away from the bed.

"I'm Seth. Zeke's my twin. But I'm the one here to have my cut feet checked."

"X-ray sent me to get Myra Maxwell for an ultrasound. Clearly I'm in the wrong cubby. But what are the odds?" She backed out with the portable bed and chart.

Seth and Lila shared a confused look. "You saw Myra yesterday at Rory's game," she said. "Come to think of it, last week Mom saw her in Dr. Rice's office." Lila patted Seth's arm. "I'll be right back. I'm going to find out." She called to Rory, too.

Seth heard a commotion in an exam room beyond Rory's. Suddenly Lila burst back into his room wearing a huge grin. "Myra and Zeke are here. Myra's pregnant. They're checking to confirm that everything is normal."

"Wow! Fast work. It's only been six weeks since they got married." Seth sat up.

"More like eight. But I think it's neat, don't you?"

"I guess." Seth lay back. "Son of a gun! I'm going to be an uncle."

A nurse led Rory into Seth's cubicle and sat him in a chair. The subdued boy rested his new psychedelic orange cast on its arm while the doctor cut away Seth's socks and inspected his feet.

"You pulled off quite a rescue," the doctor told Seth. "My nurse will clean these cuts, give you a tetanus shot and provide a pair of clean white socks.

Expect your feet to be tender for a few days. I recommend soaking them in Epsom salts. Call my office if you see any infection." He turned to Lila. "Your young man had two clean breaks, like I told you. And no sign of concussion. We'll leave his cast on four weeks then re-x-ray."

"I can't play ball the rest of the summer." Rory looked glum. "But I shouldn'ta gone to the mine." He held out the dirty white stone. "This is all I found and the nurse said it's not diamonds." He scooted the chair nearer to Seth's bed.

Seth smiled. "Not diamonds, but it's a nice white quartz. Wash it, and it'll make your mom a pretty paperweight."

The doctor rinsed at the sink, said a nurse would be right in, then left.

"Lila, your mom will lay Rory going to the mine right at my feet."

"Your poor, cut feet," she said, but dropped a kiss on Rory's bent head. "When I spoke to her, she praised you, Seth, for rescuing him. But if she reverts, Rory and I will set her straight, won't we, son?"

The boy nodded.

"Still, I'm sorrier than you know that Rory overheard my friend Yoti's call. I tried to be clear that few gem hunters find stones worth millions. It's not his fault for hoping a windfall of sapphires would let you work less and spend more time being a mom. I wish I'd made clearer that's my intention, too. We've discussed my future, Lila, but not really ours. We'd never have as much money as Kemper's folks, but by teaching and coaching I can provide for us well enough to allow you to cut back at the café," Seth said, holding Lila's gaze.

Her eyes popped. "Seth Maxwell, was that a back-handed proposal? Are you asking to marry us, as Rory might say?"

"Yes. I want nothing more than for the three of us to be a family. Never more so than when I first heard Rory's voice in that mine. I knew then that you and he are my real treasure."

Lila rushed over to drape her arms around Seth's neck, but she spoke to her son, who'd sat up straighter in his chair. "We'll marry him, won't we, Rory?"

"Oh boy! Yeah! Having a dad to play baseball with when my arm gets better is way cooler than Kemper's batting machine."

"I have an admission," Lila said soberly. "When you didn't come straight out, Seth, I conquered my fear of mines to go inside to find you. I can't explain how peace came over me right before you yelled that you had Rory and would bring him to me. Trusting and loving you killed my old dread. Seth, I love you both so much."

"I love you guys, too. Can we make us a family ASAP? Mid-July? I see no reason to wait, do you?"

"None. When we leave here I'll phone the Artsy Ladies and put them in charge of planning our wedding. And you, Rory Jenkins, can escort me down the church aisle, neon-orange arm cast and all."

"Yay! Can Memaw fix food like at Auntie Myra's

wedding? She made a yummy cake and lots of other good stuff."

Seth grinned as a nurse bustled into the room with a syringe and a basin to clean his cuts. "Rory may only be nine, but it's plain the way to his heart is through his stomach, like it is for all men."

Their shared laughter set the tone for their future.

* * * * *

COMING NEXT MONTH FROM

HARLEQUIN®

Western Romance

Available August 2, 2016

#1605 A BULL RIDER'S PRIDE

Welcome to Ramblewood • by Amanda Renee

After a stay in the hospital, bull rider Brady Sawyer can't get back into the arena fast enough. Which is against the advice of Sheila Lindstrom, the doctor who put Brady back together...and could possibly break his heart!

#1606 TEXAS REBELS: PHOENIX

Texas Rebels • by Linda Warren

Everything is changing for Phoenix Rebel. Not only has the formerly carefree cowboy discovered he's the father to a baby boy, he's also fallen in love with Rosemary McCray—a sworn enemy of his family.

#1607 COURTED BY THE COWBOY

The Boones of Texas • by Sasha Summers

Kylee James keeps people at arm's length for good reasons. Especially Fisher Boone. With her past dogging her, Kylee knows the handsome cowboy deserves happiness, which is something she could never give him...

#1608 THE KENTUCKY COWBOY'S BABY

Angel Crossing, Arizona • by Heidi Hormel

Former bull rider AJ McCreary has inherited a ranch in Arizona and the timing is perfect—he needs to get off the rodeo circuit to properly raise his toddler daughter. Problem is, Pepper Bourne thinks his ranch belongs to her!

SPECIAL EXCERPT FROM

HARLEQUIN®

Western Romance

Brady Sawyer almost died the last time he rode a bull, and now he's determined to compete again. Can surgeon Sheila Lindstrom risk her heart on a man who cares so little for the life she saved?

Read on for a sneak preview of
A BULL RIDER'S PRIDE,
the latest book in Amanda Renee's popular
***WELCOME TO RAMBLEWOOD** series.*

"This can't happen again." Sheila squared her shoulders. "It happened, we got it out of our systems, we don't mention it to each other or anyone else. I could lose my job over that kiss."

"Then, you're fired."

"I'm what?" Sheila laughed. "You can't fire me as your physician, Brady."

"Actually, I can. You're telling me us being together is an issue because you're my doctor. I'm eliminating the problem."

"It's not that simple," Sheila said. "Grace General Hospital frowns on doctors dating former patients. I'd lose the respect of my colleagues. And if you run to my attending and have me removed as your doctor, it will raise a few red flags. I put my entire life on hold to become a doctor. I'm not throwing it away for a fling. Dedication and devotion from people like me are the reason you're alive today."

"Sheila, I respect your career. I admire your dedication and achievements." If she only understood that he'd devoted the same energy to his own career.

HWREXP0716

She scoffed. “You take everything for granted. I helped give you a second chance at life. A second chance to see your son grow up, and you want to throw it all away for pride.”

“It’s not pride. I have to earn a living to support my son.” Brady sat down beside her. “Gunner is everything to me.”

“Gunner doesn’t care what you do for a living. He’s four! He loves you no matter what.” Sheila threw her hands in the air. “Okay, I’m done with this conversation. I don’t care what you do.” She stood and reached for the doorknob, then hesitated. She slammed her fist into her thigh. “So help me, I do care.” She spun to face him. “That’s the problem. I care what happens to you.”

Brady hadn’t expected Sheila to admit her feelings for him. He’d suspected and even hoped the attraction was mutual. But hearing the words, the connection between them took on a completely different meaning. How could he walk away from a woman who intrigued him like no other?

He reached for her hand. “This is all I know how to be—a bull rider. A rodeo cowboy.”

“You’re so much more than that,” Sheila whispered.

Love the Harlequin book you just read?

Your opinion matters.

Review this book on your favorite book site, review site, blog or your own social media properties and share your opinion with other readers!

Be sure to connect with us at:
Harlequin.com/Newsletters
Facebook.com/HarlequinBooks
Twitter.com/HarlequinBooks